MISS KEATING'S TEMPTATION

by

Margaret SeBastian

FAWCETT COVENTRY • NEW YORK

MISS KEATING'S TEMPTATION

Published by Fawcett Coventry Books, a unit of CBS Publications, the Consumer Publishing Division of CBS Inc.

ISBN: 0-449-50226-0

Printed in the United States of America

First Fawcett Coventry printing: December 1981

10 9 8 7 6 5 4 3 2 1

CHAPTER 1

The Home Counties originally consisted of Middlesex, Essex, Kent, and Surrey and comprised that circuit of the Judiciary which was closest to "home," London. The growth of London in size and importance soon justified extending the appellation to include the counties of Sussex and Hertfordshire. With the exception of the last two mentioned, these counties abut upon London. Although not every Englishman thinks of London and its environs as home, since a majority of them resided there, one can conclude that a majority of Englishmen found nothing exceptional in this usage.

The expansion of the metropolis filled these outlying counties with residences of those excellent peers and citizens who could not afford the time it took to travel out to their country estates in the far shires and had to settle for something close by the center of the commercial world or the center of the social world or the center of the governmental world, namely, London. The result was that all of the Home Counties could boast of housing the lights of England even as far out as Hertfordshire.

About twenty miles to the north of the capital could be found one such eminence, both of wealth and politics, the Earl of Cowper. His estate, Panshanger, was extensive and quite beautiful, having been laid out by the famous landscapist, Repton. For all its beauty, one cannot help but believe that, in these, the early years of his marriage, it was his Countess who captivated him above all else.

Emily, Lady Cowper, daughter of Peniston Lamb, Viscount Melbourne, and sister to the rising young politico, William Lamb, was as much the darling of society as she was the apple of her husband's eye. She was a beautiful and a lively lady and commanded the admiration and devotion of the beau monde to the extent that she, together with a handful of other great ladies, literally ruled society as a Patroness of what was referred to, sometimes, as the young ladies' Valhalla, the weekly Assemblies at Almack's in St. James.

The proximity of Panshanger to London, and its comfort, encouraged the Earl of Cowper, as it had done his predecessors, to invest in Hertfordshire real estate. It was a wise investment, for Hertfordshire became a prescription of London physicians when they had to recommend a change of climate for their patients. Rents rose accordingly and a goodly sprinkling of wealthy valetudinarians began to find places for themselves in the shire and with the Earl of Cowper, their landlord. In fact, the saying was current that "he who buys a home in Hertfordshire pays two years' purchase for the air."

But there were also the poor sort of invalids who could not easily afford such a prescription. Such a one was Sir Joseph Keating, Bart. As a result of some wise investments before consumption brought a close to his financial activities, he had gained for himself and his children a reasonable income. It enabled him to remove himself and his family to Tewin, but two miles from Panshanger, where a small Elizabethan house was leased to him by Lord Cowper. This plus the added expense of a young gentleman at Oxford left little for his daughter Ann and himself to enjoy. Still it was comfortable and the Hertfordshire air was a deal easier for him to breathe than that of the City. He managed to maintain the domicile of a country gentleman of modest means and was content to live out the rest of his days there.

Ann might have been as satisfied as was her father, except for the fact that, amongst her friends was one, the Honorable Georgette St. John, daughter of Viscount Olney. The St. Johns also resided in Tewin, as tenants of the Earl of Cowper, but their abode was a grand manor house, whose size, appointments, and upkeep bespoke a high level of affluence. They had a town house in London and estates in Sarum and spent only a part of the year in Hertfordshire.

It was very edifying to Ann to be numbered amongst Georgette's friends. It gave her a comprehension of the beau monde she could never have got otherwise. At the same time, Georgette's accounts of her activities served to generate in Ann a sense of panic. She was well past sixteen years of age and there was not even a hint of a prospective marriage partner in her life. Georgette appeared to have no such worries. In London, so she said, there were all manner of gentlemen who did nothing all day but languish while they waited for her to make her appearance. She could look as high or low as she chose when it came to selecting the proper gentleman.

Ann could well believe it. Georgette had beauty of person, fine family, and untold wealth behind her. It was bound to be easy for her to choose any gentleman. The very ease of Georgette, with regard to this problem which was beginning to haunt Ann, made clear the difficulty that the latter must face in this regard. She had no riches. As the daughter of a baronet, her breeding was unexceptional but nothing more, nor had she any great charms to boast of other than a neat figure and excellent eyes. With regard to the latter, she had no other person's word for it but her own. In any case, it could be said that her eyes, a clear hazel, dominated her features, adding a quality of brightness with their sparkle to give more than a pleasing effect.

Still, it was little enough to consider in light of all the attractive qualities Georgette possessed. In sum, Georgette was a beautiful heiress of the nobility, and Ann was nothing of the sort.

The problem of her future had not troubled Ann for the two years that she and her father had spent in Hertfordshire. Of late, however, things were changing, both within her and without. A feeling of anticipation was being communicated amongst the young ladies of her acquaintance and it was a feeling that she shared with them. The talk was now more concerned with style and with London and, most of all, with how each and every one of them would accomplish her coming out.

With the exception of Ann, their debuts into the fashionable world were being planned for a London occasion. Some notable female relation would be acting as their sponsor, if their own parent thought it wiser and enjoyed so valuable a connection. Otherwise, something of a ball was being planned, and at some expense, to take the notice of the *ton*, and some manner of introduction into Court circles devised to guarantee the appearance of the particular young lady at a Court function.

All of these arrangements were to be pursued with the only objective being to announce to the world that the young lady was "in the market," to put it bluntly.

The only thing that Ann found distasteful in all of this was the fact that she could have no equal part in it. At her house, there was no such excitement planning; there was no such talk of London and great doings. Considering the state of the Keating wealth and Sir Joseph Keating's health, there was just not any point in mentioning Ann's prospects. It would have only embarrassed her father, she was sure, and frustrated herself to the end that such a discussion must have been unprofitable.

In the frequent meetings with her friends, Ann's part in the conversations was to listen to everything that was said and to try to find something in it that might be of advantage to her. For the past few months, what she had heard had only turned her green with envy. None of it could help her to her heart's desire, for all of it required a degree of wealth and, perhaps, a lineage that the Keatings could not demonstrate.

CHAPTER 2

The music room of Sabine House, the St. Johns'
residence in Tewin, was larger by far than the
Keatings' drawing room and the cost of its appointments greater than the value of the Keatings'
entire leasehold. It housed, in the greatest comfort, the group of young ladies who were assembled
there, one afternoon, to continue their endless discussions of their plans for the next Season in London. They had all been invited by formal note and
so it was bound to be something of an occasion.
The fact that their hostess was not there to greet
them only added to their anticipation of what
Georgette had in store to reveal to them.

Ann, of course, was delighted to have been included. Considering how far below all of her
friends she was in social degree, she understood
their condescension and was grateful for it. Had

she not been included in their circle, she would have been at a loss to find other companions in this elegant district. To have consorted with yeomans' daughters and serving girls was, of course, quite out of the question. She had not even an abigail at home but had to make do with the services of the two maids-of-all-work who ministered to the Keatings' needs, together with a poor excuse of a cook, a local farmer's wife.

The ladies had been chattering amongst themselves for some twenty minutes before Georgette made her appearance. The smile of triumph on her face was sufficient to inform her company that, indeed, she had great news to impart to them.

In her hand she held a folded sheet of fine foolscap which she made sure to display to all by the very obvious manner in which she used it as a fan; but not a word did she say regarding it until, like the very proper hostess she was, she had greeted one and all and had exchanged conversations here and there about everything under the sun.

The ladies were fit to burst and their eyes were glued to the note she continually flourished, each of them trying to conjure up an explanation in her own mind regarding its importance.

Finally, Georgette, with a great flourish, waved it about and shook it open. At once the room came to a hush. Not even a breath was taken until Georgette announced: "My dears, I have just received the most exciting news and I was sure that you would wish to share it with me."

It was not saying very much, but the ladies had held their breaths long enough, and there was a gasp as the tension began to be relieved. They waited, impatiently, for Georgette to proceed.

"The fact of the matter is," she proceeded, "Is, ladies, that I have in my hand here, my voucher for Almack's—"

Her friends' eyes went wide with surprise and then narrowed in undisguised envy.

"But that is the least of it. My dearest mother has consented to holding my coming out at one of the Assemblies. Of course, all of you will be invited. Indeed, I should insist upon it."

For Ann the news was truly exciting. Almack's! Almack's, the goal of every lady, young and old, the achievement of few. Just as heaven on Earth is beyond the hope of all but the saintly, so Almack's was beyond the hope of all but the most select. It was a revelation to Ann that Georgette St. John should have become one of the elect, and *she* was accounted her friend. It gave her a thrill, for it was bound to be as close as she could ever get to anyone of exalted social standing.

Ophelia Anstey demanded: "Tell us how you did it, Georgette! It was Lady Cowper, was it not?"

Georgette's eyebrows rose in disdain. "I assure you it was not. It would have been no achievement at all to have gone through her ladyship. After all, we are the greatest of Lord Cowper's tenants and he could never have denied my father in this—"

"But I was under the impression that it had nothing to do with the gentlemen. It is only the ladies who have the say."

"Quite," agreed Georgette. "I have not the least doubt but that Lady Cowper would have honored my mother's request. Nonetheless, it was through the kind offices of Lady Jersey that my voucher was obtained."

Joyce Saddler exclaimed: "Heavens, Lady Jersey—but I had heard she was an odious dragon! One never had a chance with her unless one's antecedents had owned half of England since before the Conqueror!"

Everyone laughed, and Georgette beamed at the implied compliment. "Indeed, Joyce, it is quite as you say, and if the St. Johns have not owned so much of England, it is only because our gracious ancestor, Rolande St. Jean—they were quite French in those days—Norman, you know—Sieur Rolande was not a greedy man—"

"I dare say that none of the Ladies of Almack's can say as much for *their* lineage," suggested Ophelia.

"Oh, I am sure that one or two of the ladies could—at least by marriage," said Georgette, agreeably condescending.

Although Ann knew of Almack's by repute, never having been close to anyone who gained entrance to it, her curiosity was aroused and she asked: "But, Georgette, pray tell me precisely how one goes about securing a voucher to the place. I mean to say, it is a club, is it not? And it is not *owned* by the Ladies of Almack's. How do they come to say who shall enter and who shall not?"

Ophelia, her face screwed up in an expression of exaggerated surprise, declared: "Stupidity, thy name is Ann!"

Joyce exclaimed: "Well! It fairly escapes me how anyone with the slightest pretensions of being a lady can know so little about Almack's!"

"I am a lady and need have no *pretensions* upon that score!" retorted Ann.

"Joyce, that was not a nice thing to say," admonished Caroline Bentinck. "In those who have no expectations of procuring a voucher, a knowledge of the circumstances of Almack's is, at best, the result of mere curiosity. I should say, in your case, my dear Miss Saddler, it was idle curiosity, indeed!"

Then Caroline turned to Ann and said: "My dear, it is quite simple. You see, actually, Almack's is a misnomer. It is truly to be understood as Willis', for Mr. Almack has been dead and gone these many years. And the Rooms are not as exclusive as all that. Anyone with the price of their rental can occupy them—"

"I beg your pardon, Caroline, but you are quite out in your opinion," interrupted Georgette. "Almack's—yes, I know that it is actually Willis'—but what is *referred* to as Almack's is quite the most exclusive Assembly Rooms in the kingdom. Only the bluest of blood can gain admittance—"

"No, no, Georgette, you have got that quite wrong, I assure you!" said Caroline. "I tell you it is the Assemblies that are exclusive. The Rooms can be had by anyone—"

Georgette was angry. "Do you mean to imply that I am lying when I say that my coming out is to be held under the auspices of the Ladies of Almack's?"

"Not at all, for I agree with you. It is truly the Ladies of Almack's, namely the Patronesses, who have all the say. All I am trying to point out to Ann is that the Assemblies to which you refer consist of a ball given once a week in the Season.

They are the so very exclusive affairs, and I offer you my hearty congratulations that you are soon to be a member of that select group. Indeed, I envy you, Georgette. Indeed, I do!"

"Thank you, Caroline," replied Georgette, looking quite pleased.

"I pray that I shall not again cause any dissension if I ask another question but I should very much like to gain a complete understanding of Almack's," said Ann.

Very condescendingly, Georgette said: "As I am about to become a member of that august and select circle, I venture to say that I am the best person to whom you ought to address your inquiries, my dear."

"Thank you, Georgette. I gather that Lady Cowper, who is wed to our mutual landlord, is a Patroness, as is Lady Jersey. Are there any other ladies concerned in the business, and who might they be?"

"Yes, there are other ladies, ladies of the highest rank and of stainless reputation and breeding. There is Lady Cowper, and Lady Jersey, and there is—ah, let me see now— Yes, there is Lady Castlereagh, of course, and—um—ah, Caroline, I am sure you know almost as much as I do about the Ladies of Almack's. Why do you not go on with it—for Ann's sake, of course."

"If you like. Ann, why do we not retire to the next room where I can tell you all about these grand dames without our disturbing anyone—"

"No, no, you shall not be disturbing us, I assure you," Georgette hurried to interject. "I am quite sure we all of us would very much like to hear your version of it. If you are incorrect, I shall point it out."

There was a small, wry smile on Caroline's lips as she nodded. "Indeed, Georgette, I should be happy to oblige you all. If you do not mind, I shall start with Emily, Lady Cowper."

There was general assent as everyone moved themselves closer to Caroline. Even Georgette, maintaining a knowing look upon her face, gave her full attention to Miss Bentinck.

"I do not have to say all that much about Lady Cowper. She is a Countess and resides with her husband at Panshanger. I am sure you all know that and if you have caught a glimpse of her ladyship, I do not have to tell you that she is a very lovely lady. The thing is that she is very well liked by everyone and that is more than can be said for any of the other dames of Almack's. By reason of the fact that Earl Cowper is a bigwig in Whig politics, if you will pardon my pun, she cannot be easily disregarded by the other ladies.

"I should say that her opposite number among the ladies is Countess de Lieven. Actually, it is just Lieven, but everyone uses the 'de' in addressing her. She is nothing like Lady Cowper for either beauty or grace and is rather an arrogant sort; but, as she is a foreigner and wife of the Russian Ambassador, I dare say much is forgiven her. If I had any chance of being granted a voucher, I do not think that Madame de Lieven would oblige me.

"Then we come to Georgette's sponsor, Lady Jersey. Her ladyship is without doubt the chief amongst the Patronesses, and I do not think there is anyone who dares challenge her with the exception of, perhaps, Lady Holland—but that is another tale. If Lady Jersey will vouch for one, there can be no question of one's acceptance by all the finest families in the land. She is an imperious dame, from what I have heard, and has good reason to be, having inherited the Child family fortune. Joined with her husband's, the Child-Villiers must be tremendously wealthy, and it may explain why the Earl was willing to append his wife's family's name to his own. In any case, she it is who guides the policy of admittance to the Almack Assemblies.

"Of course, you know that it is all with the ladies; no gentlemen are involved in their councils; although I have been told it was not always like that. With regard to the gentlemen's costume, they did consult with Mr. Brummell, and I suppose that is why the gentlemen are under obligation to wear what is practically court dress if they are to accompany their ladies past the portals of that glorious sanctum of society.

"There is also Lady Sefton, Princess Esterhazy, and Lady Castlereagh at the present time, but these ladies do not have as much to say about things as the others. I do not mean to imply they have no voice in the doings of Almack's, it is just that Ladies Cowper, Jersey, and Lieven are the ones you are most likely to hear about."

Caroline, with a good-humored smile, turned to Georgette. "If I have left anything out, I pray you will oblige us all by adding to our discussion."

Georgette thought a bit and then shook her head. "No, I am quite sure I could not have done it better, my dear; but I am not so sure I understand about Lady Holland. She is but a Baroness and all these great ladies are Countesses at the least. Yet, you say that no one dare challenge her?"

"It is a curious thing that the Patronesses of Almack's, the three ladies who are the most outstanding at least, are all of the same age. Lady Holland is at least ten years their senior and the wife of the notable Lord Holland, a great political figure and literatus of our day. The fact that he is quite important in Whig circles speaks plainly to the fact that the Cowpers and the Hollands must be quite thick. In any case, Lady Holland has ruled society in her own way since before Almack's had been thought of. One might almost say that it would be a condescension on her part if she were to partake in the councils of Almack's. Does that satisfy you, Georgette?"

"Yes, yes, of course. I knew it all the time. I just wished to have my memory refreshed. Caroline, my dear, if ever I should be elevated to join those great Ladies of Almack's, I shall be only too happy to grant your request for a voucher."

"Thank you, my dear," said Caroline. "I shall treasure your promise to me to my dying day."

CHAPTER 3

Caroline and Ann walked home together after the visit, and Ann was pleased to have her company. She was filled with a feeling of confused injustice and had a need for a sympathetic ear.

"Do you truly think that Georgette will keep her promise to you? There was that in your tone to make one doubt it."

Caroline laughed. "My dear, I do not put any store at all in anything Georgette says. She is something less than bright you will agree, and the caliber of the Ladies of Almack's is extremely high. No, I should say that Georgette has gone as far as she can in gaining her voucher. She will add some beauty to the Assemblies but little charm."

"But what about you? Have you no wish to enter

Almack's? To me, a voucher is to be devoutly desired."

"Indeed, I do agree, but it is not worth one's time to yearn for that which is beyond one's reach. Surely, you do not think you have any chance of a voucher, do you?"

Ann sighed. "From what I have heard this afternoon, it does not seem likely, although I do not see why I should not. What does Georgette have that I do not—or *we* do not?"

Caroline smiled. "Now you are being childish, Ann. She has all that is needed for Almack's, all that we do not possess."

"I do not see that that is so."

"All right. We both of us are unexceptional ladies. I am sure our characters are as unblemished as is Georgette's; but that is where it stops. Have you anything that says you may be on a par with the highest ladies of the land?"

"Has Georgette?"

"Of course, she has! She is the daughter of a wealthy Viscount, and I stress the word wealthy. No matter what is claimed for Almack's, having a wealthy family behind one does not hurt one's chances. You will note that all of the Patronesses are extremely wealthy. Then there is the matter of birth. There is nothing exceptional about my family. We can trace ourselves back to the Netherlands quite easily, for one of my ancestors came over with William of Orange, but if he had been one of the Conqueror's retinue, that would say a deal more. Still, it is not enough. *I* am of the gentry, of good family, and modest affluence, but I am not connected in any way with any of the Patronesses other than that my family has Earl Cowper for landlord. Can you say more than that for yourself?"

Ann smiled ruefully. "Papa is not a peer, if that is what you mean, and our circumstances are modest, too, but our lineage is as excellent as the St. Johns' as far as I know. I do not see what that has to do with it anyway. If Georgette can receive an invitation to Almack's, I see no reason why I cannot, too! After all, it is just an Assembly, and we all of us have attended the Assemblies at Sabine House and at Panshanger—and those at the latter were sponsored by the Countess of Cowper, I should point out!"

"And pray, how much conversation did you have with her ladyship? Would Lady Cowper know you were she to meet you upon a street in London?"

"Perhaps that is my fault for not having brought myself to her notice."

Caroline shook her head. "So then she will know who you are, but that does not raise you to the heights, my dear Ann. You cannot doubt that Lady Cowper has many acquaintances and, perhaps, even friends, who have never received a voucher. The same may be said, I am sure, for all the other Patronesses. On the other hand, people who are perfect strangers to them, by reason of their standing in society, can easily demand a voucher and receive one. I cannot imagine, if one were on a par with Lady Holland, as an example, that any of the Patronesses would dare refuse her. In fact, I wonder what would occur if Lady Holland demanded a voucher for one of her own family or friends. Would the ladies dare deny her?"

"*Would* they dare?"

Caroline laughed. "Truly, I cannot say. They

might. They are sticklers for form and precedence. Even if you have got a voucher but forget to bring it with you, you will be denied entrance. That is how strict they are."

"Oh, I do not *believe* it! It does not make sense! It is just a bit of paper."

"For that bit of paper, my dear, there are ladies in this land who would sell their souls—although *that* is not likely to recommend them to the Patronesses, I assure you."

"Can it be all that important to one?" asked Ann.

"If you have any wish to make an excellent marriage, yes, it most certainly can make a difference. Just think of all the exalted people one can meet there. Dukes and earls, the rich, the mighty, eligible gentleman to the right of you, eligible gentlemen to the left of you. You cannot help but find yourself a husband on the highest level you could desire."

Ann walked along in silence for a while as she thought it over. Then she said: "Somehow the entire business of Almack's strikes me as unfair. I can understand why it is that not just anybody can get in, but it is outside of enough that either you or I should be denied vouchers to the place."

"Oh, have you been denied one? I have not, for the simple reason that I have never sought one. Really, Ann, I could never picture my mother calling upon Lady Jersey for the purpose of gaining admission to Almack's for her daughter. One just cannot go up to a Patroness and make a demand, you know. There has got to be some reason behind your request."

"I have a reason! I wish to marry as well as I can."

"And so do we all! I wish you great good luck in your pursuit, my dear, but I regret to say, Almack's is well beyond your reach. You shall have to do as well as you can without any assistance from that quarter."

"How do you know you would be refused if you asked?"

"Ann, truly I do not know categorically that I should be refused, but reason tells me that I should. I have not the rare blood and the even rarer accomplishments of face, figure, and pocketbook that seems to be requisite. I should only embarrass any Patroness I petitioned, and should be beyond mere embarrassment myself."

"Nothing essayed, nothing gained, Caroline. I suggest that we go to Lady Cowper and ask *her*. Everyone says that she is the sweetest of them all. Even if she were to refuse us, I should imagine she would do it gracefully and we should not be embarrassed."

"Ann, I find it difficult to take you seriously. Lady Cowper is a Countess, and I am not so brave. I am but the lowly daughter of one of her husband's tenants. Where do I come to ask such a thing of her?"

"Georgette is precisely the same! A daughter of one of Lord Cowper's tenants—"

"But it was not the Cowpers Lady St. John called upon. It was Lady Jersey. Can you not understand how that came to be? The St. Johns were not about to ask a favor of the Cowpers, their landlords, for the simple reason that they consider themselves on a par with them, socially speaking that is. By appealing to Lady Jersey, or so it appears to me, they avoid the whole business of landlord and tenant. Now, neither you nor I can have the least excuse to approach Lady Jersey or any of the other ladies, except Lady Emily—and there you have got this business of landlord and tenant, and naught else. Does it make sense to you that a landlord should vouch for a tenant to the all high, for the reason that she *is* a tenant? I think not. I think there is a deal more to it than that, and neither of us has got it."

By this time they had come to the front gate of the brick house that was Ann's home.

"I shall have to think on it," she said, by way of concluding the conversation.

"Be sure that that is *all* you do, Ann, and I will come for you tomorrow. Perhaps we can go for a stroll along the banks of the Maran."

Absently Ann agreed and they parted. Ann went into the house in search of Sir Joseph.

Ann was informed by the servants that Sir Joseph was out in the field at the back of the house. She found this rather surprising and wondered what great change had occurred. Her father was used to finding himself a seat for the day, somewhere about the house, and to never stirring from it for hours on end. That he should be out of the house and in the fields was incredible.

She came out of the back door and paused. There was his tall thin figure standing so that his back was toward her. It was an unfamiliar sight, for he was standing quite erect; there was none of that defeated look his stooping shoulders conferred upon him. Had she not known better, he gave all the appearance of a gentleman in reasonably good health. It worried her that, with his complaint, he should be out in the open without even a shawl to his shoulders and no one near to render him support.

"Papa, is that you?"

Sir Joseph turned about and smiled at her. "Of course, it is I, child. Did you have a pleasant time at the St. Johns'?"

Ann came up to him and replied: "It was most interesting, the things we talked of—but I fear I have been overlong away from you. Had you not better withdraw to the drawing room? I am sure you are overexerting yourself."

"I have been standing out here for quite some time, my dear, looking about me with a new spirit. I have been too much indoors these days and am fatigued with the existence of a valetudinarian—"

"Oh, but, Papa, what will Mr. Mallow have to say to that? I am sure he will be most distressed to hear that you have ignored all his instructions to rest—"

"I am out here because of Mr. Mallow, child! He and I have come to the same opinion. He visited me today and things have changed. Ah, it is good to stand upon one's own two legs and feast one's eyes upon God's Creation!"

"Papa, I do not understand," protested Ann.

"Come, daughter, and walk with me—unless you are too fatigued with your visiting."

"Oh, I am not at all fatigued, Papa. I should dearly love to walk with you, if you are sure that Mr. Mallow approves."

"That is what I wish to speak to you about, and I can do so as we stroll."

They began to walk through the field. Ann took hold of his hand and was pleased to feel how firm his grip was. It had been years since she and her father had walked together, and that was as long ago as their London life. To have him by her side once again, when she had been assured by the doctors in London that Sir Joseph could never again expect to be able to stand up to the least exertion, was thrilling. She could not take her eyes from his face as they went.

"According to Mallow, I should not have any appetite, considering for how long I have had to play the role of invalid," said Sir Joseph. "As a consequence, he has given my affliction a great deal of thought. His conclusion, my dear, is that I am not suffering from a bout of consumption. What it is, is something like it, but nothing to take a toll of my strength. He does not doubt but that my lungs have been affected and cautions me against a return to the smoky streets of London. He is even inclined to believe that a climate, something more salubrious than Hertfordshire's, might gain for me a complete remission of the complaint."

"Oh, Papa, how wonderful!" cried Ann.

Sir Joseph smiled. "Aye, it is that, and more. I have been forced to neglect you, and I see a chance to make it up. I understand that Brighton has all the air of a country fair, and I have no liking for the sea. In any case, Mr. Mallow frowns at the thought that I should immerse myself in salt water. Bath, I do not think, offers any greater advantage than Hertfordshire, or as much. As I recall the place, it is situated in a deep bowl and is known for an occasional bout of sticky weather, something I dare not risk. No, Mr. Mallow had in mind a location with some proper elevation, with a climate that would assist me. I mentioned Cheltenham and he quickly agreed to it."

"You wish to go to Cheltenham?" asked Ann, feeling vaguely disappointed.

"Yes, my dear. It will give me an opportunity of convalescing more rapidly and, at the same time, afford you a better prospect than any you can have, here in Hertfordshire."

Ann's disappointment crystallized, and she was suddenly aware of what was bothering her. It was too early to leave Tewin; she had things to accomplish. She had not realized it, but she had already made up her mind to it, and departing from Tewin at this stage must render all her plans futile. She needed time. She needed time to consider exactly what it was she wished to do, and she needed time to do it when she had come to her decision. Furthermore, it had to do with Lady Cowper, and at the distance of Cheltenham, she would be so far out of her ladyship's ken, it would be as though the Countess had never heard of her.

"But, Papa, must it all be so sudden? I have friends—"

"Yes, I know, my child, but Cheltenham is a charming place. I have no doubt but that you will be able to make new friends, friends every bit as charming as those whose company you now enjoy—"

"But, Papa, you are looking so well now. Perhaps Cheltenham will not be all you think it. I mean to say, I have no objection, none at all, to our removal to another place, it is just that I think it rather sudden. Surely, we ought to discuss it more fully."

Sir Joseph laughed. "Of course, my dear, we shall discuss it more fully. We shall not be moving tomorrow. There is the lease, you know. I shall have to try for an arrangement with Lord Cowper's man of business and see what can be done in that regard— But, if they will not take it back from me, it is naught to concern ourselves with. It has only a matter of months to run before its renewal. There is no rush. In any event, I should like to walk about the country for a bit. Mr. Mallow does not object to that so long as I do not exceed my powers and rest at the first shortness of breath that I experience. Would you mind very much accompanying your father about the district? Even if we do leave, I should like to improve my acquaintanceship with my neighbors. I understand that we have some very important people about besides the Cowpers and the St. Johns."

"Oh, Papa, I should love it. I cannot express to you the joy that I feel. I could kiss Mr. Mallow for it!"

"I dare say he might take a few shillings off his bill for that treat, my dear— But let us not be overhasty. Even now, I think I ought to return to the house. No, it is not my breath that is short, it is my legs grown weary. They are even less used to walking about."

It was all right, thought Ann. Suddenly the future was turned bright. Papa was going to be well and she would have her chance to mend things for herself. Although she could not see her way to accomplishing her idea at the moment, there would be time for her to find her way. Now that her father was so markedly improved, she might even discuss her prospects with him without feeling restrained from speaking lest it fatigue him.

CHAPTER 4

The little stroll had sharpened Sir Joseph's appetite so that they had an early dinner; after which they sat themselves down in the drawing room, Sir Joseph to read and Ann to embroider.

"Papa, may I speak?" she asked when Sir Joseph turned a page in the volume he was studying.

"Of course, my dear," he replied, putting down his book and looking over to her with a smile.

"Cheltenham is in the Cotswolds, is it not?"

"On the far edge, I should say."

"Then it is rather distant from London."

He pursed his lips and nodded. "Two-days' journey from the City and a bit more from this place, for we should have to go into London to find the stage, if that is how we decided to travel. But that is rushing things. I should prefer to go in our own carriage, and at our leisure and see the country-side. In that event four days might be sufficient."

"But once we were there, it would be a journey to come back to London, I mean to say."

"Yes, but I cannot imagine what would call us back to the City. Here, we are ever so much closer and have not had occasion to visit London in all the time we have been settled."

"But, Papa, if you are going to be well, surely there will be occasions arising that would require our presence in the City."

"I cannot imagine even one."

Ann bit her lip. The conversation was not going well. She racked her brain to find another tack.

"Papa, I am not getting any younger, you know, and as the years pass, if I am to wed, I shall have to find a fitting society in which there are eligible gentlemen."

"So that is what is worrying you, is it?" he said with a laugh. "My dear, I do assure you that in Cheltenham, there is sufficient fitting society to satisfy you. The place is like Bath in that it, too, has springs; but I should say it is something more exclusive in that there are more our class of people there. We both of us will be much more comfortable in Cheltenham—not that we shall be able to afford a residence within the City's limits, mind you. All such places are bound to be beyond our means. I was thinking of finding something in Swindon or Prestbury, either of which is but a stone's throw away from the heart of Cheltenham."

"Yes, I should prefer to live outside the City, but I was thinking that we should arrive in the district a father and daughter of no particular distinction and without connections of any sort."

Sir Joseph frowned and studied his daughter for a moment before he replied. "Ann, there is something bothering you, and I should like to know what it is. If you have a particular objection to the Cheltenham district, I pray you will make it plain to me. I want you happy, and heaven knows these past few years have not been easy for you."

"Nor have they been for you, Papa, but I was thinking that there is a way for us to settle anywhere we please and with something that must speak highly of us, that must unlock the doors of Cheltenham society and make us more than welcome within them."

Sir Joseph smiled slightly and said: "Your father is a baronet. That is not the lowest level of the gentry, and as my daughter, you share in my distinction."

"But as it stands, it is not enough to bring us to the notice of—a peer, for instance."

"I do not see why not; although I do not comprehend what we shall have to do with dukes and earls and that lot. Even here in Tewin with a viscount for neighbor and an earl for landlord, we have had little enough to do with them. You have Miss St. John for friend. I see no reason why you may not find in Cheltenham another viscount's daughter, or even an earl's daughter to become friendly with. But I do not see any importance in it. Such rank and wealth is beyond our power to emulate and I, therefore, suggest that you lower your sights, young lady. If it is a duke you would wed, no, you'll not find him in Cheltenham, no more will you find him in Tewin, no more you will find him in London. That sort of circle is quite beyond us, I assure you."

"Not if I had me a voucher to Almack's!" Ann blurted out.

Sir Joseph sat up suddenly in his chair and stared at her. Then he exploded into laughter. "Oh, Ann, Ann, you are such a child! There is as much likelihood of your receiving a voucher for Almack's as you have of being granted an audience by Princess Caroline. I admit there was a time when I might have enjoyed a very friendly connection with His Royal Highness, the Prince Regent, but then this cursed condition took hold of me and I was forced to quit the Elysian fields of High Society before I ever had stepped foot in them. It is too late now. I should have the greatest difficulty in reestablishing my former connections. And, my dear, without such connections there is not the smallest possibility that you would ever be noticed by the Patronesses of Almack's to any degree worthwhile."

"Is not our family the equal of anyone's?"

"Aye, it is, my dear. In that regard we have nothing to be ashamed of, but there is a deal more to it than mere family. There are quite a number of good families in England and more than most of them have no better chance than do we to get our daughters into Almack's. Now I bid you cease to think about it. I have no intention of returning to London, and what plans we may make for you cannot include a voucher to Almack's in them."

"But, Papa, we *do* have a connection! There is Lady Cowper! Is there some law that says I am not to speak to the lady?"

"There is no need for such exaggeration, my

dear. Of course, you are free to address her ladyship. She is a neighbor, and to that extent, I am
sure she would have no objection to our paying a
courtesy call upon her husband and herself when
they are in residence. But it is out of the question
that you should ask a voucher of her merely because you are neighbor to her."

"I do not see that it is exceptional. A voucher
is for the purpose of vouching for someone. As we
are their tenants and they know us, what is to
prevent them, her ladyship in particular, vouching for me?"

"It is one thing to vouch for a party in the way
of business; it is quite another when it comes to
gaining entrance to Almack's. There we are concerned with the finest families, the finest ladies
of the nation—"

"I do not think that Georgette St. John is one
of the finest ladies of the nation, and *she* has got
a voucher for Almack's."

"Has she?" asked Sir Joseph, quite surprised.
"I was not aware that the St. Johns rated so highly
with the Cowpers. Of course they are both Whigs,
and that may explain it—"

"Then it has naught to do with fine families if
that is the way of it! But it was not the Cowpers
who granted it, it was the Countess of Jersey. I
dare say that makes a difference," suggested Ann.

"Ah yes, of course it does! With regard to the
St. Johns, Lady Jersey's sponsorship is quite unexceptional."

"But, nevertheless, it could have been done just
as well by Lady Cowper. You have said as much.
Whatever the odor of it, it would have to be ac-

cepted. I mean to say Lady Jersey could not have objected to it."

"Whyever should she, child, if she has sponsored the girl herself?"

"I mean to say that, despite the fact that we are tenants of the Cowpers, if Lady Jersey was pleased to offer me a voucher to Almack's, it would be every bit as good a voucher as that which Georgette has got."

"Well, yes, it would be—but that is quite beside the point. I admit to surprise that Miss St. John has been accepted by Almack's. It is a sign to me that they must be lowering their standards for admission—but that is not to say that you, my pet, are in the same class with her, I am sorry to say—"

"But why am I not? What has Georgette got that I have not? We are of an age. Our family is as good as anyone's. You, my father, are not of the lowest gentry—"

"It is a matter of wealth, Ann. Sordid as that may sound, it is quite a sensible qualification. Just consider that the cost of a gown for you to attend one of their Assemblies would pay a half-year's rent on this leasehold, and you will see why it is essential that any candidate for Almack's must be of a family that can afford the expense. Perhaps the ladies who manage the business are bound to be high-nosed about the subject of money, but how would you like it if at a party that you gave, certain of the guests came in rags for the reason that they could afford no better? That is to carry a metaphor to an extreme, perhaps, but if you were as wealthy as, say, the Duke of Buccleuch, your appearance, that which we can afford at this point, might very well strike you as impoverished and cast a damper upon the festivities. In short, my dear, even in the highly unlikely event of a voucher being granted you, we could not afford to have you attend even one Assembly. Now, I pray that I have made it quite clear to you."

"Yes, Papa, quite clear."

If her thinking was to be guided by the counsels of her father and her friend, then all her wishes with regard to Almack's must be put upon the shelf until such time as they appeared more reasonable. In Ann's estimation, this would not be soon enough to be to her advantage. What made the prospect of immediate consequence was the fact that Lady Cowper resided but two miles away and, as neighbor, Ann had a reasonable expectancy of being received by her ladyship if she paid her a call. That much her father had admitted.

She could not gainsay the fact of her inadequate qualifications for Almack's, but that was not to say it militated against a voucher being issued to her. Just the fact that she could not afford to attend the glorious Assemblies was not, in her estimation, an impassable obstacle to the voucher itself.

Yes, she would have liked beyond anything to be able to attend the Assemblies, but she would not stick at that, and she did not see why the Ladies of Almack's should, either. What possible difference could it make to them that, having received a voucher, she did not attend? As long as she was not to reside in London, the voucher would serve merely as a token of her acceptance in the capital's society and it would serve her well when they came to live near Cheltenham. It was not all that she wanted, but it was sufficient to grant her a small part of her wish, a perfectly harmless condescension on the part of the Ladies of Almack's that must do herself a world of good.

During the days that followed, Ann was over to the St. Johns', along with her other friends, every day. Georgette was filled with her glory and had the need to allow her humble friends to bask in it. Both Ann and Caroline were more than willing to please her, so that they might enjoy the luxury of Sabine House as it had been redone by the St. Johns.

At the same time, it allowed Ann to give further consideration to her problem. She listened to every word Georgette had to say as to how the voucher had come to be granted to her. And she listened equally carefully to Georgette's plans for the great event, the details of her gown, how her hair was to be dressed; and, too, every name connected with the St. Johns' London acquaintanceship was stored in her memory.

Caroline, apparently, had long been a scholar of London Society and had made it a point to study the *Gazette* and the London papers assiduously. Whatever was doubtful or incomplete in Georgette's conversation, Caroline, when she and Ann were together, could easily correct or fill in for Ann.

All of this caused a change in Ann's thinking that bode fair to upset her recent conclusion. Settling for a voucher that she would never be able to use for lack of funds no longer seemed to be the answer. Somehow, some way she must gain a full and free admittance to Almack's. If ever there was a heaven on Earth for a young lady, it must be contained within the four walls of Almack's in St. James, and it would be a crime against nature if she were to be denied her place in the Assembly.

Caroline was no help to her with regard to how such a feat was to be accomplished. Almack's was beyond their reach and Ann had better make the best of it. She doubted if, each year, as many as fifty young ladies were so fortunate as to be invited to attend. On that basis alone, Ann must consider how far below on the scale of nobility she was. It stood to reason that any peer's daughter must take precedence over her and there were more than sufficient such young ladies from whose ranks the Ladies of Almack's could easily make their choice.

The trouble with this reasoning, from Ann's point of view, was that it did not explain Georgette's selection. Admittedly she was a peer's daughter, but beyond that fact, Ann could not be brought to see how Georgette was more qualified than herself to take the notice of Lady Jersey. Her father had indicated that he could have had the necessary connections had he not been taken ill. At least that was what she had understood him to mean. Well, there was no reason for it to have changed things. She was still his daughter, he was still the same Baronet. Just because they were not so wealthy and could not afford a London address should not count so heavily against her. This was one thing that had to be explained to the Ladies of Almack's or a gross injustice would be committed—to herself.

And, yes, she must attend an Assembly if only but once in her entire life. For this she was quite willing to live in a hovel for the half year her father said it would require. That was something she would have to take up with him. For the privilege of attending Almack's, they could forgo a house such as they had in Tewin and accept a modest cottage in the Cotswolds. An ancient shepherd's cottage could not cost so very much—and they would actually save something as they would be in London for the short time required for her to have her gown made up and her appearance at the Assembly.

The more she thought about it, the more excited she grew. It seemed so very reasonable and it all could be done before her next birthday. The Season was about to begin and she would not be seventeen for three months. Why, it could be in the nature of a coming out party, just like Georgette's!

Once Fancy frees itself from facts, its flight is boundless, and Ann, having got so far with her thinking, managed to meet at that very first Assembly the young, dashing Marquis, son and heir to a duke, who was to be swept off his feet and into her pocket at first glance. By the time she had managed to run through a most idyllic existence with this young hero, she was rather exhausted, and reality brought back to her the chilling necessity that not a bit of this fairy tale could commence until she had taken the very first step—the call upon the Countess of Cowper!

It sobered her, but it did not cool her resolve. At least she was fortunate in having to deal with the most pleasant of all the Ladies of Almack's. Caroline had reported that fact to her and it eased her mind. From what she had heard of the others, especially Lady Jersey and Countess de Lieven, the ordeal of meeting with any of them might well have been more than she dared.

At home, the talk of Cheltenham continued. Sir Joseph was becoming more and more convinced that they should remove themselves to Cheltenham. For Ann, this meant that time was growing short. She did not dare to mention her ideas to her father until she had obtained the needed promise from Lady Cowper. After all, if they were to have to sacrifice their way of life for her advancement, there had to be a certain prospect of the latter before they prepared for their life of deprivation.

So it was that, late one fine morning, Ann left Tewin and walked the two miles to the front portal of Panshanger, her heart in her mouth at every step of the way.

CHAPTER 5

There was a bright smile of welcome on Lady Cowper's lips as she said: "Come in, my dear Miss Keating. How fortunate for me that I should find myself at home when you called! It is so rare that I have even a few idle hours to spend, these days at Panshanger. But do sit down and tell me how it is with Sir Joseph. I was speaking to Mr. Mallow only the other day. Why, I do declare, I believe it was but yesterday, and he informed me that Sir Joseph's condition was confounding him, and all for the good."

The Countess was as beautiful in a morning dress as if she was attired for a local Assembly, Ann thought. There was such a youthful look about her, even though she was almost twice her own age.

Ann returned her ladyship's smile and began

to feel quite at ease. She had not expected such informality at the start.

"Thank you, your ladyship. I am pleased, nay happy, to say that Sir Joseph is remarkably improved. It is as though I have got me a new sire."

"Ah, I am delighted to hear it. I am sure it must have been a trial, for anyone can see that Sir Joseph, but for his illness, is a most dignified and worthy gentleman. And, I would add, his daughter is a remarkable young lady. I have remarked to my lord how devoted you were to your father and he, too, was enchanted to see how careful you were of him. It is too bad that his illness prevented him from going about and did not allow of his receiving callers. Perhaps, if he is so much improved, there will be an opportunity in the future for Sir Joseph and yourself to pay us a visit. I know Earl Cowper would be delighted to chat with him."

"I am sure, my lady, Sir Joseph must be flattered to hear your good opinion of him. I have no doubt but that in a little while, he will have recovered sufficiently to be able to pay his respects in person to his lordship and your ladyship."

Lady Cowper's face fell. "Oh dear, I fear we must all be a little disappointed then. My lord and I are expected in London tomorrow and, because of the time of year, I doubt if we shall return to Panshanger before the Season is over. It would amaze you, Miss Keating, how much there is to do before each Season begins. It is no secret of course that I and my friends are concerned with the Almack Assemblies, and there are so many young ladies that have to be examined for their quality. Alas, so many apply and so few can be chosen—but I do not think you would find that topic of any interest and I apologize to you for having mentioned it."

"Oh, but, my lady, I am quite fascinated to learn all that I can about Almack's!" protested Ann. "In fact, that was why I have come calling. I had a wish to speak to you about it."

The bright look on Lady Cowper's fine face dimmed and she raised a hand to stroke her eyebrow. "Really, my dear Miss Keating, I should not have mentioned it at all. Actually, I am not at liberty to discuss the Assemblies as it is all of the most confidential. I pray you will excuse me if I do not encourage a conversation in that regard."

Ann's face mirrored her disappointment. "I beg your pardon, Lady Cowper, if you take exception to my persisting, but it concerns no one but myself, that which I wish to discuss with you."

Lady Cowper smiled knowingly and shook her head. "No, my dear, you can not get round me so easily as that. You may well believe that hundreds of young ladies would die for the opportunity that you are enjoying now— But you must not forget that I am at home to you because you are my neighbor and not because I am a Patroness of Almack's."

"But if I cannot speak to you about it, my lady, whom can I discuss it with? Unlike others, neither I nor my family have any acquaintance with any of the other Patronesses. You are my only hope."

"Miss Keating, you do not seem to understand," said Lady Cowper, a slight frown gathering between her eyebrows. "It is never a question of whom you know that will gain you admittance to Almack's but who you are. You appreciate the difference, of course."

"Then it is just a matter of wealth. One has only to buy one's way—"

"Miss Keating, you are being impertinent! That is not the case at all, and for you to insist upon it to *me* is insolence. No candidate for Almack's gains admittance until she has been approved by all the Patronesses. Only so many young ladies can be approved and that is not to say that those who do not receive a voucher are in any way exceptional. It is just that they do not rank as high as those who do. It is a matter of character, charm, family, and the quality of their breeding that determines each case."

Ann wore a sullen look. She arose and ducked her head at Lady Cowper. "Before I take my leave, your ladyship, I will say but one thing. I do not believe that Georgette St. John is more deserving of a voucher to Almack's than am I. I beg your pardon for having taken up so much of your time."

"Just a moment, young lady! I do not care for your manner at all. I begin to suspect that Almack's is as far from you as the least of young ladies, nor do I see that Miss St. John has anything to do with your manner, for she has not received a voucher! She could not possibly, as we have not had an opportunity to discuss any new ladies.

"I pray, Miss Keating, that upon our next encounter, you will have mended your manner. Until this moment I had thought you a most sensible and charming girl."

There was hurt and anguish in Ann's eyes. She stood uncertainly at her chair, biting her lip. It was obvious that she was not finished but was fearful to say anything more.

Lady Cowper took pity on her and smiled. "Miss

Keating, I have no wish to be harsh with you. Come, sit down. I am sure we can find something more profitable to speak on."

"It is just that you do not understand, Lady Cowper. I beg leave to inform you that Georgette—"

"That will be quite enough, Miss Keating! You have my permission to withdraw." Lady Cowper's features were firmly set as she stood up and stared at Ann, imperiously.

Ann shook her head, turned about, and quickly left the room. She did not want her ladyship to see the tears start.

By the time Ann reached the front portal, guided by a footman, she was quite blinded with tears. But she would not wait to regain her composure. She wanted very much to flee this house where she had been so completely frustrated.

As soon as the door was opened for her, she stumbled forward into the sunlight and wound up in the arms of a gentleman who exclaimed: "I say, what have we here?"

She would have fallen from the shock of the encounter, but his strong arms quite firmly encircled her and held her safe. For a moment, she rested against him, and that pounding in her ears; she could not tell whether it issued forth from his breast or her own.

"What luck! I have got me a maid in distress, I am sure. How do, my charming maid?" he greeted her, still holding her close. Then he tilted up her face and bussed her smartly on the lips.

The fury engendered in her by his impertinence was not to be borne. Ann thrust herself from him and stood glaring at him as best she could through tear-bedimmed eyes.

"Sir, you are a cad to take advantage of me in so odious a manner!" she stormed.

He laughed and replied, "If there is some less odious fashion in which I may take advantage of you, my sweet, you have but to name it."

"Oh, insufferable!"

"After such a remarkable introduction, I am sure that courtesy demands we make ourselves known to each other."

With that he bowed and said: "I have the honor of being Henry Vassall. Perhaps the name is not unfamiliar to you, my pet?"

She had dashed away her tears, and there were none to replace them because of her indignation.

"I do not consider this any sort of an introduction, sir. In the future, I demand you will keep your distance from Miss Ann Keating, daughter of Sir Joseph Keating, which is myself!"

"Rather awkwardly put, wouldn't you say? Ah, but then the entire business is a bit awkward, isn't it. Still, I am unhappy to see tears in the eyes of a charming young lady, especially one who has sprung upon me from the doors of Panshanger. If I can be of the least assistance, my dear, do not hesitate to inform me. I cannot, for the life of me, imagine that it was Lady Emily who reduced you to such misery. Pray inform me at once who the miscreant was, and I shall belabor him to the best of my ability and make him sue for your pardon. I say, it was not Lord Peter, was it?"

Ann was quite thoroughly confused. Her mind was trying to wrestle with the problem of Lady Cowper, and this stranger was making such a demand upon her notice with his glib address that she could only stare at him, speechlessly.

He stared back at her, his poise slipping from him as was his smile.

"I say, I did not mean for you to take me seriously. I was but jesting, you know—or don't you have a sense of humor?"

"If you will allow me to pass, sir, I would refrain from any comment other than that you have a very strange way of conducting yourself with a lady you have met but for the first time."

"Ah, but it was the impulse of the moment and I am sure you will allow it. I beheld a fair damsel in distress, even tears. What could I do but staunch their flow so that we might chat and give me an opportunity to discover how I might be of service. Pretty females in tears affect me that way, you see."

His mock sincerity, and the fact that he cut a handsome figure, accomplished his stated purpose. Ann found herself smiling at him.

"Ah, that is so much better," he said, and he took out a handkerchief for her to dry her eyes.

"Now then," he chirruped like some schoolmaster, "if we are feeling much improved, perhaps we can examine the cause of our distress."

At the reminder, Ann's face clouded. "It is Lady Cowper," she murmured.

"Emily? I find that difficult to believe! Emily is the sweetest and most inoffensive of persons. Are you quite sure?"

Ann nodded. "She would not listen to me. All I wished was that she should grant me a voucher for Almack's."

His eyebrows lifted. "Oh, I say! I thought it was something quite serious."

"It is!"

"Oh, not Almack's! It is a most deadly place. I cannot imagine anyone actually wishing to visit it."

"Mr. Vassall, I have already been through this with her ladyship. I see no point in continuing the debate with you, sir. I pray you will let me pass."

At that moment, a footman came out of the house and said: "Your lordship, the Countess will see you now."

Lord Blayde made a face and replied: "Bid my lady to be patient. I have urgent business to attend."

A look of horror came into the footman's eyes. He said in a disapproving tone: "If that is what you wish, your lordship."

"It is."

The footman went back into the house.

"Who *are* you?" demanded Ann.

He smiled down at her and said: "I dare say I forgot to mention I am Viscount Blayde. It is apparent that you have not heard of the Vassall family. It is a lack in you, my dear, if you aspire to enter through the portals of the holy of holies."

"I had not understood that a knowledge of the peerage was necessary."

"I am not saying it is, but it would help if you had acquaintance with the leaders of society. Perhaps I can help you to it."

"Then you are a leader of society? Is that why you are here to speak to Lady Cowper?"

"Good lord, no! I cannot imagine anything so utterly boring. I have the misfortune of being Lady

Holland's distant cousin and so I am dragged into all manner of petty businesses. At the moment I think that I am supposed to be delivering a message from my relation to the Countess. Except for the fact that Lady Emily is so devilishly attractive, wild horses could not have brought me out here."

Ann stared at him for a moment. It seemed to her that the conversation verged upon the ridiculous. She had never met with a high-ranking nobleman who maintained such an unaffected manner. She was even more astonished when he clasped his hands behind his back and made a little bow to her, saying: "You see, Ann, I am very eligible and they like to keep their eyes upon me."

"Your lordship, I fear that you mock me," she said.

"Indeed I do not, Ann. I merely wish to help you, if that is possible."

"But it is in the hands of Lady Cowper and she has given me a flat refusal. I do not see that anyone can help me now, for I do not know any of the *other* Ladies of Almack's."

"Ah, but you know *me!* Is Almack's so all-fired important to you?"

"You know it is, my lord! It is every maiden's devout desire to be included in at least one of those extraordinary Assemblies."

"Extraordinary is hardly the word, my dear—and I would not object if you called me Henry. I mean to say we are thoroughly introduced by this time, and one might even say that we were on intimate terms with each other. Consider what might be made of the little salute we exchanged but moments ago—"

"I did nothing of the sort! It was you—"

"It matters not, my dear. If it had been witnessed, I have no doubt that my eligibility would be somewhat impaired."

"That is perfect nonsense! There is absolutely not a thing between us and you know it very well!"

"I know it, for you have just said it, but the world does not know anything of the sort."

"Oh, but you are a fool. If it will set your heart at ease, I will assure you that I shall not breathe a word of it to anyone," said Ann, disdainfully.

"How awfully unkind of you. Here you have been kissed by Viscount Blayde and are completely unaffected by him."

"I would not go so far as to say that. But however I may be affected by you, sir, is something less than flattering, I must say. Now, I think we have talked nonsense long enough and I have got to return home."

"Yes, I do agree. Allow me to see you there. Where is it?"

"I abide in Tewin. It is but a stroll from here, and I would not dare to request your absence from Lady Cowper. I am sure that she can treat with you a deal better than I can."

He laughed. "I am not inclined to agree, my dear. Perhaps it is something we can discuss further as I drive you home in my curricle."

"And then perhaps not—"

"Oh, but I insist! There is still the business of Almack's to be worked out."

"My lord, you carry a jest too far. I was sure we had agreed that there was naught that could be done for me in that direction."

"It was you who stated it as a fact, but I never

agreed. Actually, it is quite the easiest thing. A bit of skill, a bit of daring, and I have no doubt that I can grant your wish."

"That is an idle boast."

"That remains to be seen. My trap awaits your pleasure," he said, pointing to a glistening little vehicle that looked much too flimsy to require the exertions of the team of bloods harnessed to it.

Ann regarded it for a moment and then said: "Thank you, my lord, but despite what you have said, we are not at all acquainted and it would be most exceptional in me to accept a ride in a strange gentleman's carriage."

"I swear to you I am the soul of honor and virtue. With such a relation as I have got, I have no choice."

"Who is fool enough to give oneself a *bad* name?" said Ann, shaking her head.

"Are you not being overnice about the business? It is but a short ride and we are out in the open in broad daylight. Good heavens, girl, what are you afraid of?"

"It is only common sense. It just is not done, nor is it approved of. If you are so hot to discuss the matter further, my lord, then I suggest that we walk together out on the public highway. In that way there can be no objections from anyone."

"There most certainly can be—from me! Do you expect me to walk in *these* boots? Do you have any idea what they cost me—and the pain I should have to endure? I assure you they were never made for walking along rough, rural lanes."

"That must certainly assure your good behavior I am thinking," said Ann with an impish smile.

"I should not have the least trouble in fleeing from you if I saw the need."

He grinned. "Indeed, and I shall instruct my cordwainer of the problem with the next pair of boots I order from him—but, in the meanwhile, I suppose we must walk, mustn't we?"

"If you wish to accompany me, my lord—but I do not see the necessity. I am quite sure you cannot make good your claim about Almack's—and, besides, why should you even wish to go to the trouble for me?"

"Say it is because of my fondness for you, my dear— Or, say it is because I would teach you a lesson. Almack's is bound to be a disappointment to you if you have any sense. To prove my point, I needs must see to it that you have your look-in at a typical Assembly."

They had passed out of the gates of Panshanger and were walking along the road.

"I should be forever grateful to you, my lord, if you should succeed."

"Oh, I shall succeed. Never doubt it, but there are conditions that you must agree to before I begin."

Ann drew herself up and declared, angrily: "My lord, you have come far enough with me. I have no wish to hear your conditions, nor to have your company."

"The devil you say! My poor feet are suffering an ordeal of agony with every step! I am not about to turn back at this point for what it has cost me to come so far! You will listen, my pet, and obey!"

Ann glanced down at his boots and considered her position. They did appear to be quite dainty and cramped for walking about, considering how tall Henry was.

"Very well, but I warn you, sir, at the first insulting allusion, I shall leave the spot on the instant and never stop until I am safe at home."

"I have no doubt of it. The condition consists of the fact that, as we are about to enter into a conspiracy together, it seems to me that we should be upon better terms with each other—"

"My lord, I am poised to flee!" warned Ann.

"Allow me to finish what I have to say, blast you!"

"Very well!" she snapped back at him.

He shouted: "I want you to call me Henry! I think it is fitting!"

"Very well, *Henry!* Does that make you happy?" she shouted back at him.

They broke into laughter as their idiocy dawned upon them.

CHAPTER 6

They had been walking together for some minutes. Although the day was warm, the road was lined with trees and Ann, used to strolling about the countryside, was quite comfortable. Every now and then she looked up into her companion's face, a question in her eyes.

Lord Blayde's face was tight. His eyes were narrowed and his lips pressed closely together. Ann was beginning to feel sorry for him. It was obvious to her he was in great discomfort.

"Would you care to stop and rest for a bit, Henry?" she asked.

"Gad, no! We have hardly walked. Oh, I say, if you are fatigued, of course we can stop."

"No, I am not at all fatigued. I am quite used to walking; but as you are not—and you have all the appearance of one in great pain—"

"Pain? Me? Not a bit! Oh, you are thinking of my boots, are you? I dare say they could be more comfortable but I am not limping yet, so there is naught to worry about."

"But you look as though you are suffering," she persisted.

"I tell you I am not suffering!" he replied, shortly. "I am trying to think, and if you will be quiet for a moment, I am sure I shall have it."

"Is it the voucher? But you seemed so sure you had a way to gain one for me. I am beginning to think it was all a ruse."

He smiled at her. "Indeed, it has served as an excellent excuse for me to enjoy your company, but I am no blackguard. Of course, I have got a plan. That was not difficult at all; it is the details that require working out, you see, and they are rather sticky to deal with."

"I do not see how the plan can be an easy one if the details are difficult. So long as the details are difficult, the plan itself must be so."

"If you are going to fall back upon feminine logic, then of course you can never begin to comprehend the business. I pray you leave it to me. A little more thought and I am sure I shall have got it all worked out."

"As we are almost halfway to my home, Henry, I suggest that you write to me whenever you get it worked out. Even though I shall be too old to have any use of it, I should admire to hear how well you have done."

"The trouble with you, my girl, is impatience. You are too impatient, and that will not serve you in this case. Nevertheless, if it will cause you to cease your clamor, I shall tell you of the plan.

Perhaps, together we shall be able to work out the details."

"I very much doubt it, but what is your plan?"

"My sister, Horatia, holds the key."

Ann appeared to be encouraged. "Oh, does her ladyship have a say in the decisions of the Ladies of Almack's?"

"No, not at all, but she has got a voucher, you see. That is what makes it all so easy."

"I do not see how. I have a friend who has got herself a voucher, and I have an excellent notion that she could not do a thing for me—if she were of a mind to."

"Oh, it is not Horatia who will be required to do anything for you. It is her voucher."

"But it is *her* voucher!" exclaimed Ann, impatiently.

"I know it is! I just told you so! The fact that it is her voucher says nothing to the possibility that you could use it."

"Nonsense! She would never permit it! They would drum her out of Almack's if they got the least wind of it—to say nothing of what they would do to me. As long as I lived, Almack's would be debarred to me—and probably to my daughters as well, if I ever had any."

"All I claimed was that it was an easy plan; it was the details that were difficult."

"It is no plan at all for the simple reason it is quite impossible."

"If all you can do is to magnify the objections and the difficulties, it is bound to be impossible. You have got to have faith and put your mind to it. Now, before you offer another sour comment, let me present you with some facts, my dear. My lady-sister, at this particular time, happens to be visiting with friends in Jersey. It will be much later in the Season before she returns. Now I can lay my hands on the voucher at any time I care to for I know where she keeps it."

"Henry, you are speaking to no purpose! It is not my name on that voucher, so how can it possibly serve me?"

"Oh, that is not at all difficult to explain. Have you never been to one of their Assemblies? No, of course you have not! Well, the thing of it is that the only one who actually peruses the voucher is the chap at the door. I admit he is a sharp-eyed lad but as Horatia has not made her appearance there yet, he cannot possibly know her. Now then, if you come into Almack's upon my arm, presenting a bit of paper vouching for you as my sister, he is not about to make any objection, for he knows *me* well enough. If I am not objecting to you as my sister, the Honorable Horatia Vassall, how can he possibly? You see, that is easily got over."

"Perhaps, but once we are within, surely the lady who *signed* the voucher would know of the substitution."

"That is not the difficulty either. Lady Holland procured the voucher for her. Of course, such a request from her ladyship would never be denied by any Lady of Almack's, and so it was not. It is doubtful that they will recognize you as not being Horatia if you do not fling yourself upon their notice."

"I assure you, Henry, if ever I got so far within those vaunted portals, I should be as quiet as a mouse. I would not dare to show myself from behind your back."

"Good girl! So you see the plan as far as we have gone is not all that impossible. Now, where it begins to stick is what do we do about Lady Holland and Lady Cowper. That I have yet to puzzle out."

"Of course, Lady Cowper would know me in an instant!"

"And, of course, Lady Holland would not. We shall just have to make sure that neither of them are in attendance upon the evening I take you to Almack's—"

"Good heavens, but that is impossible!" exclaimed Ann.

"You are doing it again! You are being defeated before you have got into the mill. It is *not* impossible. We have just to don our thinking caps and go to work."

"Then I bid you inform me precisely how I am to make my way to London upon a particular evening when, for all I know, I may be in Cheltenham when the time is ripe?"

"Cheltenham? What the devil are you doing in Cheltenham? The Assembly is in London."

"Henry, we are discussing this business in vain. My father is a convalescent and unable to travel to London. In the meantime, as he is showing signs of improvement, he is planning to remove us to Cheltenham. It was never my idea to actually *attend* the Assembly, but if I could have got a voucher, it would have added to my position in the new society of Cheltenham, you understand."

"I say! That is quite a different row! I cannot *give* you the blasted voucher."

"Precisely. Lady Cowper was my last and only hope. I thank you for your kind intention, Henry. Perhaps you will come out to Cheltenham one day and tell me about Almack's," she ended, plaintively.

"Ann, the prospect is not all that hopeless, I assure you. If your father has plans for Cheltenham, we shall just have to ask him to postpone them."

"I am sure he would be only too pleased. Imagine what he would say to his daughter making use of another party's voucher!"

"Has he no ambitions for his daughter? Many an excellent marriage has been made at Almack's," Henry pointed out.

"I am sure he knows all about it. But he is the soul of honor and would rush me off to Cheltenham if but a breath of what we have been discussing reached his ears. Actually, I ought to be ashamed of myself for even listening to you."

Henry shrugged and kicked at a stone nonchalantly. "If that is the way it is with you, I admit there is no hope at all—not that your parent need ever hear about it, of course."

"And pray how is it to be hidden from him? I should have to request his permission not only to attend, but I should need his leave to go to London in the first place."

"Does he not have any business in the City and you can join him there? Once in London it would be the easiest thing—"

"Oh, that is not at all possible! I told you he is a valetudinarian and quite unable to travel very much. As it is, he will have to regain a deal more of his strength before we are able to go to Cheltenham."

"Excellent! Oh, I beg your pardon! I did not mean it was good to hear about the health of your father—but his condition does admit of us having some time to complete our plans."

"Plans? I have yet to hear one word of these plans of yours that makes any sense—"

"Well, you are continually tearing them down as fast as I put them up! If you would just allow an assumption or two, I am sure we could get it all together and worry about the sticking places after."

"But we cannot even begin to start. Don't you see that I cannot possibly attend the Assembly if I cannot get to London?"

"Let me think on that for a moment," said Henry.

This time it was Ann who shrugged. She said nothing and they walked on in silence.

Henry finally stopped and put a hand on her arm. "I have got it! It is truly so simple!"

"Like your mind, my lord," she responded drily.

Henry looked aggrieved. "That is not a nice thing to say when you consider how I am racking my brain to come up with a satisfactory solution to our problem."

"I appreciate your kind concern, sir, but it is my problem, not yours—nor do I understand the reason for your taking the trouble."

"It is my problem as well as yours because I have made it so. As for my purpose, it is simply a bit of a challenge, and I should like to see those high-nosed Ladies of Almack's given a set down. They have had things all their own way and it is time that someone changed it about."

"It sounds quite childish to me," remarked Ann.

"Here now, young lady, do you or do you not want a look in at Almack's?"

"You know I do—but I see no progress toward that wished-for improbability—"

"Because you will not give me a chance to think! Now, listen to this: Did you notice those beasts of mine in the drive at Panshanger?"

"A very beautiful pair, I thought."

"And fast upon the road, too; but I have another pair in my stables that can trot circles about them. They are not beauties but they go like the wind. The roads out of London are rather good for the most part and it is not over twenty miles, nothing but a smart dash for the pair. If we were to travel late in the evening when there are very few on the roads, an hour and a half, all-out, would see us in St. James—"

"But what good is that if my father refuses me—"

"Oh, devil take your father—I beg your pardon! That is not quite what I meant. It is only that your father does not have to know. I assume his condition demands that he rest. Once he has retired, I can come for you and have you at the doors of Almack's and back before your household rises, and with all that, you would still have an hour or two to spend at the Assembly. There, I told you it would be quite simple if you but gave me a chance to work the business out."

Ann sighed. "It is no use, I tell you. For one thing, I have nothing to wear to so grand an affair and I should stand out like a sore thumb. For another, it would be scandalous. Why, if we were discovered, it would be taken for an elopement and my reputation would be ruined. No, I thank you, Henry, but—"

"Ah, I see what it is! You do not trust me! Ann,

after all that I am willing to undertake for you, for you not to trust me is painful indeed."

"I assure you, Henry, it is not that at all. I am thinking of what it would mean to the both of us should we be discovered in this. I am sure it would quite break my father's heart, and you will admit that your relation would have something to say to you, too."

Standing in his dignity, Henry replied: "I assure you, I have taken all of that into account. There is no risk to it. We shall be in and out before anyone has the slightest notion of anything irregular. If you had the least feeling for me, you would agree to it. Just think what it would mean after we had carried it off! What fame!"

Ann gave him a queer look and said: "I begin to think that this escapade means more to you than it does to me. In fact, I truly regret having brought any part of the business to your notice."

"What a sorry attitude to adopt! I am only trying to grant your wish, you know. I have answered all of your objections so that I have a perfectly clear conscience. The final say is up to you."

They had arrived at the gate to Ann's house where she stopped and turned.

"I thank you, Henry, for having brought me home. I would ask you in but I am not sure that my father is receiving at the moment. If you would like, I could inquire."

"Thank you, no—but I should like to have your answer. Shall we do the business?" he asked, eagerly.

Ann looked up at him and great indecision flooded her mind. It would be her only chance to visit Almack's, but it was such a risky thing to do—and then there was Henry himself! The thought struck her that it was not so much a question of trusting *him*, but rather could she trust *herself* with him. During this short term of acquaintance, she was becoming aware that the gentleman had affected her. She had a wish to see him again and she knew that unless she took advantage of his offer, it was very unlikely that they would ever meet again.

She raised her eyes to his and she said: "I shall have to have time to think upon it, Henry."

His face fell. "But it was all your idea!" he protested.

"Not by half! All I wished for was a voucher. What you have come up with is a deal more. I never contemplated actually attending an Assembly. Truly, I have got to think it over."

"Very well. I shall come by tomorrow and pay a call upon your father. I pray you will have an answer for me then."

"I promise you I shall."

CHAPTER 7

It was a dismal day in Berkeley Square. The air was laden with moisture which it dropped, at the least excuse, upon everything it contacted. The trees lining the square collected the aqueous deposit, converted it into heavy drops which dripped down through the budding branches so that each tree had its own little shower.

There was enough chill in the air, this gray afternoon, to call for lit hearths, and the soot issuing from the chimneys was quickly coated with water and deposited upon the streets, the sides of buildings, and what had been bright, highly varnished carriages drawn up in front of No. 38.

Within the smaller drawing room of No. 38 Berkeley Square, the atmosphere was completely different. Here were gathered a group of ladies, clothed in the latest fashion, and who wore expressions of aristocratic aloofness. They were all of them conspicuously conscious of the momentous occasion that had brought them together under Lady Jersey's roof, to assist in their perennial effort to maintain the purity of the highest altitudes of English society. These were the Ladies of Almack's and, in the comfort of their warm, dry, and well-lit surroundings, they were about to discuss the qualifications of the current crop of applicants for admission to the Assemblies at Almack's.

Coffee, tea, and chocolate were at their disposal as they sat and chatted about their affairs, worthy of any discussion, that had occurred between the Seasons. It was as though, before any of the business which had brought them together could be discussed, each of them had to reestablish her standing with the others, and, of course, her right and privilege to be a member of that company.

Finally, Lady Jersey knocked gently upon the little table before her and called out: "Ladies! Ladies! It is time we applied ourselves to the onerous burden that we all of us, out of our concern for the maintenance of manners, morals, and breeding, have willingly assumed. I bid you pay attention now so that we may proceed. As your president, I should like to put before you a motion to which I have given a great deal of thought.

"Upon a recent occasion, Lady Holland sent to me a request that a niece of hers, the Honorable Horatia Vassall be admitted to our ranks. Of course, I had no thought of refusing, for we all know that a request from Lady Holland is on a par with a request from any of us. Since this is so, I do not see why Lady Holland is not included amongst the present company for the purpose of assisting us in our purpose."

Inquired Countess de Lieven: "My dear Sarah, is this a proper motion?"

Lady Jersey peered at the Countess and replied: "My dear Dorothea, you know that we have resolved never to keep minutes of these meetings and, as this is not a Parliamentary proceeding, I am sure we need not concern ourselves with such imbecilities as proper form and precedent. I am suggesting that Lady Holland be invited to join us and that ought to be sufficient to further a discussion of the merits of such a proposal. By the way, I wish to compliment you ladies upon your discretion. Over the past Seasons, it has never come to my ears that anything of what we say here is being passed on as gossip to the *ton*. I think it speaks well of our devotion to our purpose—and it does go to make us feel free to speak our minds. I do not have to point out to you how restricting it would be if we had to watch everything we said. I am sure that free discussion is a prime necessity if we are to do our work with the excellent taste and discrimination that it calls for."

"I think not," said Lady Cowper.

Lady Jersey's eyes opened wide in horror. "Emily, do you contradict what I have been saying?"

"Only in regard to Lady Holland, my dear. If she had any wish to be a part of these discussions, she had only to ask. I suggest that she has as much to say about things as all of us put together."

"Well, I am not so sure of that, my dear," retorted Lady Jersey. "I do not say that the lady is not without power in these matters, but Almack's reigns supreme—"

Lady Sefton, somewhat older than the others, broke in to say: "My dear Countess, it is not to the point. Lady Holland knows no equal in her own circle, as we do in ours. I am sure that, just as we would never refuse a request of hers, she would honor any of ours. Now, I do suggest that we get on with it. I have not had my afternoon nap and am inclined to grow cranky as I grow weary."

Lady Jersey smiled sweetly at her and nodded. "Indeed, my lady, you make a telling point. If we are all agreed, we shall get on with it."

Without waiting for a concurrence, the Countess of Jersey proceeded to take up, from a list before her, the names of various young ladies. So long as some one of them was acquainted with the family, the applicant was fully discussed, all reports and snatches of gossip concerning the young party were thoroughly aired, as well as her antecedents and the current repute of her family.

Few received the stamp of approval. Those who did invariably could be vouched for by at least one of the ladies for being of spotless reputation and of a family that was either too powerful to be ignored or of sufficient rank and wealth to prove an added jewel to the Assemblies.

Occasional questions of social embarrassments were evaluated for lack of taste and deportment and the rule: "Where there is smoke, there is fire" was invoked quite frequently to disqualify more than a few young ladies.

As the list proceeded, Lady Cowper's pretty brow was seen to develop lines of concern. They grew deeper as Lady Jersey proceeded with her list. Finally, after more than two hours of argument and concession came to an end, she shook her head and interrupted Lady Jersey who was on the point of bringing the meeting to an end.

"Sarah, I do not think we have examined all the candidates."

"Ah, have I missed someone?" Her ladyship raised her eyeglass and peered at the list in her hand. "No, I do not think so, Emily. See, I have checked each and every name upon the list as we disposed of them."

"That is my point, Sarah. The name was not on the list. I do not say it belongs there, but I heard, from a source that is not necessarily to be relied upon, a voucher may have been issued to a young lady who was not included in today's conversations."

"Of course, that is always a possibility. I am sure we all are guilty of it, every now and again; but when one is so certain of the qualifications in a case that is personally known to one, there is little need of introducing the name into these sessions—"

"Not, my dear Sarah, when the candidate is personally known to me, is in fact the daughter of a leaseholder of Cowper land, and, actually, my very own neighbor."

"Ah, but of course, you have reference to Georgette, Lord Olney's daughter, a dear girl, and so very pretty. I did not see the least harm in sending her a voucher. They are a very fine family."

"I have nothing to say against her, but then there are many other young ladies whom we rejected, and there was naught to say against them either."

"Ah, but there was the difference, my dear Emily that *I* thought it unexceptional to provide a voucher in this instance. I am sure that my judgment can be relied upon in this instance," replied Lady Jersey, the faintest tinge of color in her cheeks indicating her growing indignation.

Lady Emily's eyebrows were lifted as she said: "Still, it would have been an act of courtesy to have informed me of your action. As it is, in my ignorance, I have been guilty of basing a refusal to another young lady upon the fact that Georgette St. John had not been issued a voucher."

"Oh, I should have got round to informing you, my dear; but I do not see that it is all that important. Those are hardly grounds to base a refusal upon. After all, you are perfectly free to submit the young lady's name to this body and we can examine into her qualifications."

"And reject her out of hand, as we have done so many."

"Emily, I do believe you are beginning to lose the spirit we are at pains to maintain in these discussions. I assure you, had I not already issued the voucher, I should have listed Georgette with the others for our approval. In any event, she was bound to be approved, so there was no point to it, you see."

"Then if I were to issue a voucher to this young lady upon my own cognizance, in light of your own action, you could not object."

"Well!" exclaimed Lady Jersey, looking about her to garner support, "as we are all gathered together, you need hardly go to the trouble. You are perfectly free to submit the name of this young lady to us, and we shall pass upon it—"

"No, I do not think so. I was odiously short with

the young lady, and I am under obligation to make it up to her, since she was in the right. As both of the young ladies in question are known to me personally, and as I should have put Miss Keating up for admittance before I would Miss St. John, upon my own prerogative, I am bound to issue a voucher to Miss Keating."

"Miss Keating?" asked Lady Jersey. "I doubt that I ever heard of the family. What, if any, is their distinction, may I ask?"

"Sir Joseph Keating, her father, is a baronet and a tenant on the Cowper estates in Hertfordshire."

Lady Jersey turned to Countess de Lieven. "Dorothea, be a dear and consult *Debrett's Baronetage*. We ought to know something more about the family, I think—unless there are those among us who can say something to that effect," she ended, looking about her at the assembled ladies.

No one offered any comment and the description in *Debrett's* was duly consulted.

There was a look of great patience upon Lady Cowper's face, but her dark eyes were glittering.

There was not much to be said for the Keating baronetage. Countess de Lieven expressed the opinion that the others did not wish to voice.

"For the family, there is not much to say. I would not waste my breath. It is ancient, but who is this Sir Joseph Keating, where are his estates?"

"That is not pertinent, my dear Countess," replied Lady Cowper. "He is a gentleman of the first water and, at present, incapacitated by infirmity—"

"He is old?" asked Lady Jersey.

"No, merely ill—"

"Ill, do you say? Really! I mean to say it was one thing to be indisposed. I am sure it is not unstylish in one to be indisposed upon occasion, but to be *ill!* How *démodé!* And I do not suppose the poor creature has a farthing to his name?"

"Sarah, they are not affluent people but they have a reasonable independence—"

"My dear Emily, you must see how impossible it becomes! Why the girl would be completely out of place at Almack's. In fact, we are doing her a favor in not granting a voucher. They could not afford the expense of her first appearance, I am sure, so it would be an utter waste of a good voucher—"

"That, my lady, is for the Keatings to decide. As far as I am concerned, if Miss St. John is deserving a voucher, then Ann Keating most assuredly is—and I owe it to her!"

"Emily! Emily! There is no cause for such heat. More is at stake than a debt to a young lady. You can make it up to her some other way. Remember, the future of the finest families of England is at stake in what we decide. Until now, there has never been a breath of scandal connected with Almack's and it is our duty to see that our reputation remains unblemished. To admit a pauper amongst our ranks— Well, I ask you, what will be *said?* No, Emily, we must be impartial in our judgments. The risk of a bad character must always be our first concern."

There was a tight little smile upon Lady Emily's lips as she shook her head. "You have said nothing to dissuade me. Ann Keating will be as much a credit to Almack's as any of us. In the event that she finds she does not belong there, I assure you,

76

we can leave it to her to make that decision. I do not believe that she has a wish to suffer embarrassment any more than the rest of us do."

"Then you are bound and determined to invite this person into the hallowed ranks of Almack's, despite anything we might say against it?"

"Indeed, I am."

"Then I have only this to add, my dear. If Almack's should suffer for it, if this person should prove to be far below the choice of young ladies in our society, you will have only yourself to blame as you see all that we have worked for, all that we have endured for, come crashing down about your feet. You, Countess Cowper, will have rendered English society a classless, odious horror, a veritable democracy such as has been created in that poor specimen of ignoble society, *Our Late Colonies!*"

As the ladies were taking their leave of their hostess, Lady Sefton came over to Lady Emily and smiled at her.

"I do think that Sarah carries things a bit too far at times, my dear. But, in the long run, I am sure it is a good thing, or we should have a most undistinguished association at Almack's. However, in this case, I think she is wrong and you have as much right as she to give a voucher where your judgment is so favorable. Actually, I am quite impressed with your impassioned defense of this Ann Keating and shall look forward to making her feel quite at home. When do you think she will attend? Perhaps I can call upon her beforehand."

"How good of you to offer, Isabella! But she is not in London, nor do I understand that she has any intention of visiting the City. Her father speaks of removing to Cheltenham, you see."

Lady Sefton laughed richly. "Oh dear, then it was all a ruse to get Sarah's goat!"

"In a way," said Lady Cowper smiling. "I thought to get my own back on her for Miss St. John—but then I was harsh with Ann and I must make amends to her. It would be sheer cowardice for me to evade the necessity of handing the voucher to her. I must needs, upon my next return to Panshanger, call upon her and deliver the voucher into her hand with my apologies."

"Ah, then it will not be soon, I take it?"

"I fear not. Affairs shall keep me in the City for quite some time. But never doubt it, Ann Keating shall have her voucher."

CHAPTER 8

When Sir Joseph had come down with his ailment, Ann had not experienced a sense of injustice. Although it was unfortunate and a cause for sorrow, it was in the nature of things that people sickened. As there was no appeal except to the arts of the physicians, one had to make the best of it.

This she had done, drawing closer to her father, assuming more of the management of their affairs then was usual for a young lady of her age. Sir Joseph was cognizant of her assistance and her care, and came to respect and admire his daughter as an individual rather than just his offspring.

Now that Sir Joseph's condition was ameliorating, he wanted her company more than ever, and so he was pleased to receive Viscount Blayde when he called.

There was nothing remarkable in the conversation that ensued between the two gentlemen, but they each affected the other in interesting ways. Sir Joseph was honored that a gentleman of rank should seek him out, and more than pleased to listen to him report on the latest doings of the fashionable world. On the other hand, Henry Vassall was impressed by the complete lack of resignation in Sir Joseph's manner. The Baronet freely discussed his condition with the young man, but not in a way to plead for sympathy. In his circle, Henry had met with many a valetudinarian and was under the impression that most were particularly enfeebled in spirit as well as body.

This was emphatically not the case with Sir Joseph. The Baronet exhibited great patience, but his determination to improve, now that his physician had granted to him the possibility, was very impressive. In fact, Henry was somewhat taken aback at the quiet authority Ann's father displayed. It gave him qualms to think about how things might go if he were to merit the disapproval of the Baronet, and that he must surely do if he placed Ann's good name in jeopardy. What had at the outset appeared to him to be a mere prank, suddenly became a most serious matter, one that rapidly lost the slightest appeal for him. Therefore, he was careful not to permit Ann any opportunity to revive their previous discussion, taking his leave rather abruptly.

While Sir Joseph complimented Ann upon having made the acquaintance of such a fine, upstanding gentleman, her mind was busy with reviewing Henry's behavior. That he had suffered a change of heart, she had no doubt, but she did not understand the cause of it. At the moment, it was just a puzzle to her, one that could be easily dismissed, as she had not intended to accept his offer. She was never so desperate as all that, she thought, and, besides, there was still a chance that she might be able to gain Lady Cowper's ear for a fairer hearing than the one she had been given.

It struck her that when she had called upon her ladyship unaccompanied by her father, Lady Cowper was bound not to pay serious attention to her. Now that Sir Joseph was able to get about, and as he was in the process of calling upon his neighbors to show them how well he was progressing, Panshanger must surely be one of the calls he was planning to make.

Since she had not informed her father of her visit to Lady Cowper—she had carefully avoided all mention of it when Henry had called, and *he* had not thought to bring it up—it was very likely that under the guise of her father's calling upon the Cowpers, she might find an occasion to mention Almack's to Lady Cowper under circumstances that would beg a serious consideration of her interest.

After a few days of walking about the countryside, Sir Joseph, after a hint or two from his daughter, thought to pay a call upon the Cowpers. Aside from attending to the amenities, he had a wish to consult with the Earl, or his man, with regard to the termination of their leasehold in Tewin.

Both father and daughter dressed for the occasion, mounted up in their modest tilbury, and Sir Joseph, himself, took up the reins for the first time in years. It was obvious that he had lost little of his skill and they drove round to the Cowpers without incident.

But only disappointment awaited them both at the portal of Panshanger. They were informed that Lord and Lady Cowper were in London and not expected back for the duration of the Season. If they would care to leave a message, it would be forwarded to his lordship, the Earl.

Sir Joseph was not in any hurry and thought to postpone his business with the Earl until his return. Ann was quite pleased with his decision because she wished to give her own little problem some greater thought. In line with that feeling, she inquired of Viscount Blayde.

It appeared that no knowledge was had of the Viscount's whereabouts. He had gone off to London with the Cowpers and the servants had no reason to expect him back in Hertfordshire.

The disappointment that overtook Ann at the news was a surprise to her. It seemed that she had been counting on another meeting with the Viscount and had not realized it until it was plain to see she might never meet with that gentleman again. It gave her more food for thought as she and her father turned out of the Panshanger drive.

Sir Joseph was beginning to enjoy having the reins in his hands and suggested that they drive into Hertford, just to have a look at the town. Ann had visited the ancient borough seat for the purpose of shopping many times in the past and took pleasure in her father's interest, acting as his guide on a little tour of the place.

They examined the Castle ruins and went on to inspect the municipal offices which had been but recently erected in the past thirty or forty years. Hertford had the air of being a very healthy, respectable, and improving town. Besides the Sessions, the Market-House, and the Town Hall, there was a good Grammar School and the Blue Coat School with accommodations for more than five hundred children.

On the basis of a slight acquaintanceship with a mutual friend, Sir Joseph took the occasion to pay a call at Brickden Bury, the home of a Mr. Morgan.

Mrs. Morgan received them, assuring Sir Joseph that he was known to them and that only the press of business had prevented herself and her husband from calling upon him. In fact, she was pleased to hand to Ann an invitation to a dancing party that she was sponsoring at Brickden Bury before Mr. Morgan and she planned to return to London for the Season. No, it was but recently that their attention had been drawn to the fact that the Keatings were practically neighbors, she assured them. In fact, it was another mutual friend, a certain Viscount Blayde, who had mentioned them.

Of course Ann was quite pleased to receive the invitation and accepted it with a look at her father. He nodded and said he would consider it an honor to escort his daughter to the affair, making no mention of his health.

Ann's excitement was short-lived, being replaced with unhappiness, as Mrs. Morgan went on to infer that, of course, they could not be happier to hold the party. Their daughter, Josephine, and the Viscount got along so very well together. Ann gathered that Henry then would attend but that she would find it quite out of place to bring up anything about Almack's with him.

Then Mrs. Morgan insisted that they take a turn about the park which surrounded their house, since they would not be able to see it so well the night of the party.

They took their leave of her, promising faithfully to inspect the grounds.

The little tour did nothing to raise Ann's spirits. The Park was well forested and had many quiet little pools scattered about to add to its beauty. It was very well cared for, too, and together with the fine house bespoke an abundant wealth, far beyond anything the Keatings possessed. The Viscount's interest in Josephine Morgan, at least until she had seen the lady, could easily be explained upon the score of Brickden Bury alone.

By the time Ann and Sir Joseph had returned home, any enthusiasm she had had for the Morgan party was completely evaporated. Having accepted, she knew that she would have to attend, but she was sure it would prove to be a dull affair.

Sir Joseph was altogether pleased with the fruits of their little outing. It was not since London that he had attended even a small supper-party. The prospect of a dance, although he would not be able to partake of the activity upon the ballroom floor, raised his spirits, and he assumed his daughter was looking forward to the party with the same pleasure.

The day had fatigued Sir Joseph, but not to the point of exhaustion. He was pleasantly tired and fell asleep after dinner, with his newspaper only partially read, while sitting in his chair in the Keatings' drawing room. Ann had no wish to disturb him and, as the evening was quite young, she left the house for the short walk over to the Bentincks' place.

Caroline was quite happy to see her and they retired up to her bed-chamber to talk.

There was a look of earnestness in Ann's face that led Caroline to believe that something was not all fair weather with her friend.

"It has been days since we have had a chance to chat. I dare say you have been busy."

Ann nodded and replied: "Rather. Papa is coming along quite rapidly now and has a wish to go all about the Shire. Today, he quite managed to tire himself out and I left him asleep. I may not stay too long, but I thought that we could talk about all that is happening. Did you receive an invitation to Brickden Bury?"

"Do you mean the dancing party?"

"Yes."

"Of course. Everyone has."

"I suppose that Georgette will be there," said Ann.

"Oh, I think not. She has left for London with her parents for the Season's opening of Almack's, and I do not blame her. I should gladly trade Brickden Bury for Almack's."

"Oh, Caroline, how I do envy her! And it is so unfair!"

"Unfair? I should think so, but that is the way of life. We have gone over all that before."

"No, that is something else. You see, I had a talk with Lady Cowper—"

"You did not!"

"Indeed, I did— But it was of no use at all. I suspect that I only succeeded in antagonizing the Countess—But the unfairness of it all was that she would not believe that Georgette had been issued a voucher—"

"That is odd! Do you think Georgette was telling us a Banbury tale?"

Ann shook her head. "You have just said that she was off to London—and we did see the voucher with Lady Jersey's signature and crest. No, it *is* odd, but the oddness is that Lady Cowper did not know of it, you see. The unfairness of it was that her ladyship would not listen to me, gave me the distinct impression that I was making up a tale to catch her attention—"

"But that is not at all like Lady Cowper, Ann! Are you sure that there was not some misunderstanding?"

"Believe me, Caroline, it is precisely as I say. I am in bad odor with her ladyship, and what is worse, I have no chance of clearing myself with her. Papa and I went over to Panshanger today only to find that Lord and Lady Cowper were gone to London for the Season."

"Oh, then that cannot be so bad," declared Caroline.

"It could not be worse!" retorted Ann.

"Oh, but you are not thinking clearly, love! Lady Cowper will surely discover Georgette at Almack's and then she will know that she ought to have listened to you. I am sure that, upon her return to Panshanger, you will shortly receive a summons to call upon her, and all will be well. She is that sort of person."

Ann looked abashed. "I never thought of that.

But then, it will be too late. The Season must be quite over when she returns, and I shall have gone off to Cheltenham with Papa. I shall never get a voucher!"

"Surely, you did not think you would, did you? Lady Cowper may be all that is sweet and kind, but a voucher for Almack's is not the sort of thing that a young lady may request. Oh, Ann, you did not ask her outright, I pray!"

"Why should I not have? I have no one else to speak for me."

"But that is precisely the point, you simpleton! Any female worthy of Almack's has at least one sponsor, if not many. Do you not understand how that very lack must tell against you? At least, if you had an aunt or the powerful friend of a friend to say a word for you with one of the Patronesses, you might be put on a list for consideration. And, if you ever managed to get that far along, you have cause to be extremely pleased as you would still be a member of a very select group. The ladies who just missed admittance to Almack's are not much greater in number than those who gained it. It is something of an accolade to have even been considered."

Said Ann, apropos of nothing at all: "Viscount Blayde will be there."

"It is as good a guess as any. Whoever he may be, he will be but one of many such at Almack's."

"No, I mean at the Morgans'."

Caroline shook her head. "That still says nothing to me, my dear. Who is Viscount Blayde?"

"He is Henry Vassall."

"A relation of Lady Holland?"

"Yes, and a very fine and handsome gentleman."

"Indeed! You have met him?"

"That day I called on Lady Cowper, and then he came to call upon Papa and me."

"Ann, how very interesting! Pray tell me more! How old is this fine and handsome gentleman?"

Upon witnessing her friend's intense interest, Ann was beginning to regret having brought Henry into the conversation; but, as there was no way to drop the subject, she went on, carelessly: "Oh, something older than we are—but there is no call to glow with excitement, Caroline. I am sure that it is the Morgans' daughter that brings him out. Are you acquainted with Josephine Morgan? I have not had the pleasure."

"No, they have been a bit high in the instep. It was a surprise to me to have been noticed by them. But what difference does it make, my dear? I am sure that we shall all have an opportunity to dance with Viscount Blayde, and for Hertfordshire, that must be counted a very great entertainment."

Ann smiled. "But I should like to discuss with you something the Viscount offered to me."

Caroline, a smile of anticipation on her face, settled down and replied: "My dear, I am all ears! I thought there was more to your coming than the foregone conclusion of Lady Cowper's reception of your petition. Now, what of this Lord Blayde?"

Ann recounted to Caroline what had been offered by the Viscount, and she did so with an anxious air. When she had done, she looked at her friend, questioningly.

"My heavens!" exclaimed Caroline, her eyes

sparkling. "And upon such short acquaintance? Isn't he the rake!"

Ann felt disappointed. Obviously, for all of Caroline's amusement, there was no note of approval in her remarks.

"Yes," she said. "Of course, Papa would never have approved and so I had no choice but to reject his proposal." She sighed. "It is too bad, for that must have been my only chance to get within the portals of Almack's, I am sure."

Caroline shook her head. "My dear, I admire you. I am not at all sure that I should have had the strength to refuse such an attractive offer."

"But of course you would have!" protested Ann. "Such brazen behavior must bring down the bitterest censure upon one's head—"

"But just think of the pleasure you would have had! What are a few sniffs of disapproval to such a dashing escapade? No, Ann, I am not at all sure I could have turned the Viscount down out of hand, especially as you say he is quite handsome. How many chances shall either of us have to spend an evening in the company of a Viscount, to say nothing of being received upon the premises of Almack's?"

"Nonsense, Caroline, you are out in your thinking! Your parents would be horrified. Why, I am sure they would lock you in your room for ages after such disgraceful conduct! To go off with a man in the middle of the night is far beyond the bounds of respectability. It could never be condoned, no matter what the reason nor the outcome."

"And I should not blame them—providing they had discovered it. If this Viscount Blayde can conceive of such an entrancing plot, I am sure its discovery must be of the utmost importance to him to prevent. See, he has even thought of your masquerading as his sister. That speaks well of his cleverness—but, what particularly disturbs me, is why he should go to such pains for a lady he has just met?"

"Well, we were very friendly together and he was filled with sympathy upon hearing of my disappointment with Lady Cowper. I suspect that he is not all that respectful of the idea of Almack's. To him it was all of a lark. You know how young gentlemen are about these things."

Caroline knitted her eyebrows.

She remarked, in a very sober tone. "It does make the business rather difficult of accomplishment, the distance to St. James being so great."

Ann laughed insincerely. "That is the least of the difficulties, I am sure."

"Oh, but there must be some way! I do not think I should ever have a restful night for thinking of this marvelous opportunity that was lost to me."

"Of late, I have not been sleeping too well for thinking on it—but what is there to do? *He* says it is but a dash to London for him and his trap!"

"Of course, such an attractive gentleman is bound to be top o' the trees with a carriage," Caroline agreed. "Truly, Ann, you must give the gentleman's proposition some great thought—and, if there is anything I can do to help you in it, I should be pleased to do so."

Ann turned thoughtful. "Yes, if I had a bit of help at this end, I might be able to manage something— Oh, but it is beyond thinking! I mean to say Papa is no slouch when it comes to being watchful for my reputation. How am I to evade his attention? There is just he and I in our house. My absence is bound to be noticed within the hour of my departure."

"Noticed, of course, but it could be allowed and approved as well, my dear. I am sure it is the simplest thing to arrange."

"I do not understand how that could be managed," said Ann with a frown.

"Just let your father believe that you are spending the night with me, don't you see? That will provide a pretext for your early departure and with sufficient clothing for the trip. Say you will be staying with me for a day or two, that we propose to attend Mrs. Morgan's party together. I am sure, as Sir Joseph is bound to be fatigued from his condition, he would be only too glad to give his consent."

Ann's face fell. "Until that point, it was a very good idea, but the thing of it is that Papa is quite looking forward to the party. He has every intention of carrying me there himself. You see, he is recovering remarkably fast and every little excursion is a treat for him who has been a stay-at-home for so many years."

Caroline's features mirrored her disappointment. "Indeed, I am so happy for Sir Joseph to learn that he is improving, but alas, it does put a very large spoke in your wheel so to speak."

"Yes, it does, and I dare say we ought to let the matter drop, it is so utterly hopeless. I thank you from the bottom of my heart, Caroline, for your friendship in this instance."

She sighed and Caroline joined her in looking very disappointed.

CHAPTER 9

As far as Ann was concerned, her little conversation with Caroline was all that was needed to put her dream of Almack's to rest for ever. There had been the one instant of joy when it had seemed there was a way to accomplish it. The intense disappointment that followed on its heels quite erased all her ambitions and she was no longer willing even to dream about the matter.

Caroline appeared to understand her change of heart and their conversations from that point on were solely concerned with the affair to be given at the Morgans'.

At home Sir Joseph's enthusiasm for his first adventure into polite society after these many years remained at a fever pitch which, for a short time gladdened everyone's hearts, not excluding Ann's. It was such a sight to see her father forever smiling as he went about directing their house-keeper with regard to which of his clothing he wished to have freshened for that auspicious occasion. But, alas, the fever pitch turned itself into a fever of another sort and Mr. Mallow had to be sent for.

The local medico was not at all surprised that Sir Joseph had suffered a setback, but he was at pains to explain that it was not in any way a relapse into his former affliction. He assured everyone a bit of rest with some hearty nourishment and Sir Joseph would be back on his feet in a few days.

Such encouraging news brought the Baronet to quick agreement with regard to the physician's prescription and, in Mr. Mallow's presence, he assured his daughter that the two days preceding the party were all that he needed to restore his fitness as her escort. To this Mr. Mallow most emphatically disagreed. He explained quite carefully that by a few days he meant something like a week to ten days of bedrest and that Sir Joseph must put all such nonsense out of his mind or suffer what might well turn out to be a true relapse.

The look of anguish which appeared upon Sir Joseph's face quite tore at his daughter's heart. Ann could not help wondering if the disappointment at missing the party would do her father more harm than good, but the doctor was adamant. In Sir Joseph's weakened condition, despite its great improvement over what it had been, the slightest chill, the slightest excessive exertion, the extra bit of warmth to be expected at a party where many people were congregating—he did not bother to spell out the doom, but his expression said all that was necessary. Both Sir Joseph and Ann resigned themselves to the fact that Sir Joseph would not be able to attend the Morgan party.

After Mr. Mallow had departed, Sir Joseph sat with Ann and they talked.

"Papa, I do assure you I am not in the least put out. Of course, I should have adored to make my appearance upon the arm of the father I revere and love, but I should much rather have that arm to depend upon through many more years than to see it placed in the least sort of jeopardy for my pleasure."

"Yes, my darling, I know your heart in this matter; still, it irks me that you must attend by yourself. If only I had not acted the schoolboy! Why, one might have thought I had never attended a social function before, the fuss I was making and the trouble I was putting the entire household to!"

Ann smiled. "Oh, do not blame yourself, Papa. We were all of us as guilty as you. We ought to have known better and insisted upon you not overdoing. Truly, Papa, it is not so important that I attend. I would much rather stay with you. I could read to you and see that your posset was prepared precisely the way you prefer—"

"Nonsense, child!" exclaimed Sir Joseph, frowning. "We shall have none of that, I assure you! You may be at ease. I shall conduct myself in accordance with Mr. Mallow's orders and you shall have not a thing to worry about but how lovely you will look and how to find room on your program for all the dances that will be requested of you. By the way, do you think that that likable young man—er, what's-his-name, will be there? I was rather impressed with him."

"Ah, I dare say you mean Lord Blayde."

Sir Joseph smiled shrewdly. "The very gentleman! I did not think you had forgotten him."

"As you know, he is expected, but one hardly dares to put credence in the prospect. He has not shown his face in the neighborhood for more than a month and I do not know that there is any great attraction for him here."

"I miss my guess if that should prove to be so, love. A young man's fancy is a most unreliable thing at the best of times, and there was talk that the Morgans' daughter had her cap set for him. I suggest that that is precisely what this affair is pointed towards—an opportunity for the two young people to get together, don't you think."

"That *is* what Mrs. Morgan implied to us when we called upon her, Papa; but I am of the opinion that Lord Blayde is something of a harebrain, and like a hare, does not himself know in which direction he will leap next."

"That is your opinion of the gentleman, is it? I am disappointed, for I had the distinct impression that there was a deal of determination in him. I did not think he was a gentleman to be easily turned aside from his goals whatever they might happen to be."

Ann laughed. "Oh, I'll grant the determination. It is the *steadiness* of his purpose that I doubt."

"Really? I had not thought that you had got to know him so well."

"Oh, you are not to take my remarks about Lord Blayde all that seriously, Papa. That is all they are—idle remarks."

"Then you will be cordial to the gentleman if you should meet with him again?"

"Whatever is on your mind? Papa, do you have the intention of throwing your only daughter at his lordship's head? I tell you the Morgans are already about to do as much for Miss Josephine, and I should come off poorly in any comparison."

"Now, Ann, I am not throwing you at anyone's head, if that is any proper sort of expression; and as for Miss Josephine, never having met the young lady, I cannot have a word to say against her. Still, that does not prevent my saying that my daughter will stand comparison to anyone. No, I most certainly am not throwing you at his lordship's head; but that is not to say I should discourage his interest in you if he should be so minded. Ann, it is just that sort of fine gentleman who might prove himself worthy of you, and it is my heartfelt regret that I shall not be able to be with you and encourage such an interest."

"Oh, Papa, things are not done that way nowadays! It is entirely up to the gentleman, I assure you, and I should be embarrassed beyond bearing if you were to say or do anything of that nature."

"Bah! It is always the same! You young people think that things have changed because it is your time, but I assure you it is a very old story indeed. Of course it is usually the mother who plays the role. As you are bereft of that advantage, it is my duty to stand in her place for you."

"Papa, I should prefer that you do not."

"It is not worth discussing, my pet. As I cannot be there, it shall have to be up to you."

In some consternation, Ann exclaimed: "What must be up to me?"

"Why, what we have just been discussing—how you handle matters with Lord Blayde, of course."

"For heaven's sake, I am merely going out to a party at a neighbor's. I pray you do not expect me to return betrothed to a nobleman."

Sir Joseph replied with a smile: "No, it need not be a nobleman, but a wealthy gentleman of no particular rank would not be a disappointment to me."

Ann laughed.

"Very well, Papa, if that is what you wish, I shall present myself to any and all of the eligible gentlemen at the party, my object clearly stated: matrimony."

He raised one eyebrow and frowned with the other. "Yes, I am sure that should gain you some attention. Oh well, my dear, I am sure that we shall have another, and perhaps better, opportunity once we are removed to Cheltenham."

Ann sighed and nodded. "Yes, perhaps so," she agreed.

The afternoon of the following day discovered Ann wandering aimlessly about the garden behind the house. It was to be the very next evening that the Morgans' party was being given and she was finding it difficult to instill enthusiasm in her heart for the affair. She was bound to be very much on her own there, having no one, not even her father, to escort her. True, there would be all the young ladies of the neighborhood attending so that she would have company, but there could be little doubt that Georgette St. John and Josephine Morgan must hold the center of the stage, the former because of her rank, the latter because she was the daughter of the hostess.

If Henry Vassall was to be there, truly, it was hardly likely that he would have more than the briefest of moments to spare for conversation with herself. And beyond Henry, as far as she was concerned, there was no interesting gentleman worthy of great attention to be found there. She was well acquainted with the brothers of her friends and the other local young gentlemen likely to have been invited, and the prospect of holding conversation with them was not in the least stimulating to her.

She had had a thought to decline the invitation but never expressed it to her father. Sir Joseph was unhappy enough that he could not go with her, and he would be disconsolate, she was sure, if she gave him any reason to believe that his indisposition was a cause of disappointment to his daughter.

As she put out her hand to touch the velvety petals of a yellow rose, she heard the rear-door of the house open and close. She turned about to greet her father only to find that it was not Sir Joseph standing there but Viscount Blayde himself.

He was smiling at her but did not advance. "I pray I am not intruding upon you, Ann. Sir Joseph gave me to understand I should find you here."

"My lord, what a surprise it is!" she exclaimed smiling and coming forward. "No, indeed, you are most welcome! But what brings you here? I thought not to lay eyes upon you until tomorrow night. You are attending the Morgans' party, are you not?"

"Why that is what I came here to find out, my dear," he replied meeting her more than halfway and taking up both her hands in his.

Ann blushed with equal shares of pleasure and of discomfort, biting her lip at the very warm effect his touch had upon her. She smiled and cocked her head.

"What, pray, did you come here to find out, my lord?"

"Dearest Ann, I did not make this trip all the way from London with any expectation of being entertained by the Morgans. I came out because, if you had come to a conclusion on what I had proposed the last time we met, this affair must provide the very best opportunity we could hope for. Actually, when I saw the marked improvement in your father's health, I was momentarily at a loss. I mean to say I was highly gratified that Sir Joseph should have grown so hale in the short time since last we spoke; but I was also aware that his presence at the Morgans must put *finis* to our little plot. I had not counted on having to elude him you see."

"But Papa may not attend. He has got to rest," Ann pointed out, frowning.

"Yes, so he has just informed me—and that put the heart back into me. It will be so much easier to accomplish that way, you see."

Ann's frown grew deeper. "My lord, that you would take advantage of my beloved parent's poor health is unspeakably odious!"

Henry conferred a queer look upon Ann. "I say, the wind has certainly shifted. If anything, the last time we discussed the business, your beloved parent was in far poorer condition than he is now—and furthermore, I am not taking advantage of anyone; I am merely trying to grant a favor to his daughter."

"Yes, but it is not one he would permit!"

"Only because he would doubt that I could carry it off. He would spare you embarrassment, but so would I, and I do have the skill to see to it; you can spend an evening at Almack's and no one will be the wiser."

Ann slowly shook her head. "My Lord Blayde, I cannot countenance it. As it must be carried out in secret and in all stealth, it is a most exceptional undertaking, one that a daughter who honors and respects her father would not dream of. I, who have thought a great deal on it, already suffer great guilt. Sir Joseph, whom I do love and honor, deserves better treatment from his daughter."

Lord Blayde snorted. "Stab me if I have not proved an utter fool! The only reason I came out of London, and it appears to be no reason at all! Ann, you are an ungrateful wretch!"

"What are you saying, my lord? There are the Morgans who have invited you. They are the true reason for your coming."

"The devil they are! Whose idea do you think it was that they ought to give a big party, inviting all their neighbors to it?"

"Yours? Oh, I cannot credit you!" retorted Ann. "Why, it was not until Sir Joseph and I happened to drop in upon them that they ever knew we existed."

Henry grinned. "I was well aware of that. But had you not been brought to their attention, I should have insured it. I am a great hand for important details."

"Oh, the entire business strikes me as being utterly distasteful."

Henry threw up his hands. "Then it is truly all for naught. I came looking for enthusiasm and all I discover is discouragement. Ann, my word upon it, I came only for the purpose of escorting you to Almack's, and I do assure you it is not your *best* chance, it is your *only* chance."

Ann was filled with great misgivings as well as disappointment. At her first sight of Henry, her heart had given a bound and she had listened earnestly to what he was saying. As she came to understand what the attraction was for him, whatever feelings she had concerning Almack's faded. It was not her as a woman that had brought him to her, but only the foil that she could be to provide him with a lark. It was the same feeling she had had concerning his interest before and he had not changed. Now she was more certain than ever that she wanted no part of him, nor did she wish to share the same roof with him.

"My lord," she said with great dignity, "it is with regret I learn of the trouble you went to under the mistaken impression that you were about to confer a great boon upon me; but I cannot countenance the business and I am not flattered to think that you assumed I should."

"Egad, now you would make me the villain of the piece! I say, we are not speaking of some dark and bloody deed. It is merely an innocent escapade, one of those capers that everyone winks at if it is done successfully."

"Ah, and if it should fail and we are found out?"

"Why talk of the improbable! We shall not be found out! I am not green. It is not a thing more than I have done many a time. So long as no one is hurt, I do not see what there is to discuss. You expressed a dear wish to visit Almack's. Out of the kindness of my heart, I went to the trouble to arrange it all— Here, let me show you something!"

He drew out his wallet and took from it a folded paper. He shook it out and handed it to her.

Ann took it and read it quickly. Even as she understood that it was a voucher for the Honorable Horatia Vassall, Henry's sister, the entire aspect of the discussion underwent a change. They were no longer speaking of what might be done but rather of what could be done. This small but powerful note in her hand was the key. She bit her lips as she stared at it, deep in thought.

There was a calculating look in Henry's eyes as he stood patiently by, quite willing to let the voucher accomplish what, thus far, he had not been able to.

Ann took a deep breath, her eyes still fixed upon the paper in her hand. Yes, she thought, it *could* be done. But could she live with herself after? There was the rub. Could she ever again look into her parent's eyes without blushing for shame?

She did not understand that her decision had already been made until she tried to return the voucher to Henry. Then it became crystal clear! Not only did she find that little deed impossible, but her mind was immediately flooded with the thought that she might never see Henry again if she finally refused to be a party to this romp. It was something of a surprise to her, how heavily this latter fact counted with her.

Still, how could she face her father? It was not a rhetorical question at this point. She needed an answer and truly believed that she could find one.

She did, and it was quite simple by her lights. Once she had returned, she would not keep the escapade a secret from Sir Joseph, but she would frankly inform him of what she had done and with all remorse, accepting without murmur the punishment he saw fit to impose upon her. She was sure that, by the time they had been removed to Cheltenham, all of it would have blown over. She would have achieved her fondest wish and nothing of it would be carried along with them to their new domicile. For the period of unpleasantness she must endure, the pleasure of Almack's was more than worth it.

She looked up at Henry and smiled. "Are you quite serious when you say that you have no other purpose in coming out to Hertfordshire but for this undertaking?"

He thrust out his chin and snapped: "Quite! If you decline, I shall leave for London immediately."

"And the Morgans who have spread it around that you will be attending, have you no thought for their embarrassment?"

He folded his arms across his chest and said, firmly: "None whatsoever."

"In that case, out of the goodness of my heart, I see that I have no choice but to accept your offer. As a proper neighbor, I must save the Morgans the embarrassment of your absence."

His eyebrow shot up.

"And," continued Ann, "there is the further consideration that I have no escort to the party."

He smiled and held out his arm to her. "My dear, I should be delighted to do the honors. Perhaps we can begin to discuss the enterprise in detail as we stroll about this charming place."

Ann placed her hands on his arm and they began to walk.

"I say but tomorrow evening is going to be quite smashing!" he crowed.

Ann prayed that he was right.

CHAPTER 10

It was a narrow road and it was dark. To all but
the traffic upon it, it must have been quite the
most courteous road in the kingdom, the manner
in which it gently twisted and turned to avoid
infringing upon the homesteads that were strung
along its banks. For all his vaunted driving abil-
ities, Lord Blayde was having quite a time of it
to make any sort of progress.

"I tell you it is much the faster route! If it was
not so devilishly dark, we would have made the
London road an hour ago," he muttered through
teeth gritted from exasperation.

Huddled beside him, Ann remarked, in acid
tones: "If you have said it once, my lord, you have
said it a thousand times. At this rate, we shall be
lucky to see London in tomorrow's daylight—not
that it much matters. We are leaving behind us

such scandal and mortification, we might as well continue the elopement over the Channel and into France. Even Bonaparte's welcome could be no less warm than what I shall have to face upon my return to Hertfordshire. A very fine plotter you are! You could not have done it worse if you had tried."

"Ann, I assure you, we shall get to Almack's before they shut the doors. It cannot be later than nine, and we have until midnight. I do assure you, once we get onto the London road, sixty minutes later you will be setting your foot upon that famous threshold."

"So you have been saying, my lord, but it seems to me that we have been upon this ungodly lane for hours and, but for your assurance to the contrary, I should take my oath we are quite lost."

"Truly, it is not as bad as that. I ought to have gone by way of Ware instead of striking down into the country—but it is such a saving in distance, this route."

"But a tremendous loss of time, my lord. Nonetheless, it is as I said: Nothing can happen at Almack's to make up for the loss of reputation I have already suffered at the Morgans'. Had you any need to be so obvious? To have come upon the floor and veritably snatched me out of my partner's arms in the sight of the assemblage was not, to my way of thinking, either subtle or clever. Then, too, there were all the dances that *you* were down for. You were the guest of honor, the center of notice; how did you dare to think that you could elope with me and no one would be the wiser?"

"Oh, dammit all, cease your nagging! How was I to know it would turn out like that! Country affairs are well under way by eight o'clock, I was sure. Nothing had actually started and it was already time to depart. I *had* to do something or we should have missed our chance!"

"I am inclined to believe, my lord, we have already done so. The way rumor travels about these days, at Almack's they will greet us with the news of our elopement."

He urged the horses on to greater speed and, in the dark, one of them immediately stumbled. With an oath, he brought them back to the crawling pace.

"Now see what you made me do!" he snapped. "If I press the beasts harder, we shall risk laming one or both of them. If you have a wish to get to Almack's tonight, I suggest you keep your comments to yourself!"

"I should just as soon return home. I cannot see that, with your handling, we shall succeed in reaching London in time. And the sooner Sir Joseph and I depart for Cheltenham, the sooner will this night be forgot."

"There!" he cried. "The London road at last! Now we shall fly!"

With that, he brought his horses about to the right and urged them into a ground-burning canter which threatened the stability of the slight vehicle.

"My lord! What on earth do you think you are doing?" cried Ann, in great alarm as with one hand she pressed her hat to her head and, with the other, kept her skirts from flying up. It was a natural precaution even though the carriage lamps shed little light within and the still air of night was not so very disturbed by their passage.

"Oh, put a stopper in it! Miss Keating, you are the last person on earth I should ever offer to assist—"

"Then we are in perfect accord, my Lord Blayde, for I am the last person on earth who would ever accept an offer of assistance from you again!"

"Bah! If that is how you feel, I am quite prepared to stop the curricle and let you down to go where you wish. As for me, I am determined to make London and in the time I promised. I am a man of my word!"

"Plague on your word! And this latest is like all the rest from you! It is no choice you give me at all. I have not the vaguest idea where we are at this moment. How should I find my way home, I ask you?"

"I do not see that it will help you any, but we have just passed through Wormley and, if I can maintain this pace without mishap, another forty minutes or so ought to see us entering the outskirts of London. I am sure of it, because I have done the distance many a time in the past."

Ann was silent for a time. The carriage flew along under Henry's guidance and, considering the utter lack of illumination, she could not help but be impressed with the speed with which they were traveling.

Still within her there was a very dissatisfied feeling. As far as secrecy was necessary to the success of the undertaking, there was no hope. The entire neighborhood was aware of something scandalous between Lord Blayde and herself, and she was sure that more than a few of her acquaintances would make it their business to apprise her father of what had gone forward.

She was not at all anxious to make explanation to Sir Joseph, knowing that she could never justify her action. If she was to insist, she did not doubt but that Henry would carry her right home. The trouble was she did not see what that would save; so things, unpleasant things, might just as well be put off for as long as they could be. All was in a shambles, the very worst was expected of Henry and herself. Perhaps, by continuing on to Almack's, making the visit there, it would mitigate the entire business. It would prove that it was merely an escapade and nothing to call forth such drastic condemnation as a truly shameful purpose would deserve.

Although this consideration permitted her to allow the enterprise to continue, it did little for her peace of mind. Henry's driving did even less.

They were on a broader highway, and the late hour and the darkness guaranteeing that traffic on the road would be practically nonexistent, Henry had put the horses into a fast canter, having his hands full to keep the animals from breaking into a gallop, now that their blood was aroused. At any faster pace, Ann was sure that the little vehicle must put its wheels into the air and expire, and she along with it.

Henry must have been having something of the same fear, for he was working like a madman with the reins.

"My lord, I pray you will slow us down a bit. I have something to say."

"I wish you would save whatever it is you have to say for later. These devils must be attended to, and I have to devote all of my skill to them."

"*That* is precisely what I would remark on, my lord," she retorted.

Henry swore as he pulled up on the reins and brought the horses down to a fast walk. "At this rate, Miss Keating, we might just as well give it over. I know precisely how much time we have got to get to Almack's before they close the doors, and it will call for our best efforts all the way if we wish to be within them when the porters swing them shut."

"The point is that, at this rate, we shall be discovered in the morning senseless or worse alongside the road, and then everyone must think the worst of us. If I am to die, I prefer to do so with my name spotless, my lord."

He turned to look at her, and he grinned. "I fear, Miss Keating, it is a little late for that. Once we have gone off into the night together, the damage is done. Our only hope is to get to Almack's. Now, it is become our only haven that will protect your reputation."

"Yes, I quite agree. So I have been thinking. All the more reason then for us to arrive at Almack's in one piece."

"And in time, or we shall never be able to explain," he commented. "So you have got your choice, my dear. An easy ride into London, surrendering all hope of preserving our fair names, or a mad dash, at the risk of life and limb. I elect the latter, for if we fail in it, once dead, it makes little difference what shall be said of us. Now, I have work to do and I would appreciate your holding your tongue until we are safely within the portals of Almack's."

Ann could find nothing to counter his reasoning.

It was very similar to what she had been thinking herself.

"Yes, my lord," she replied in a small voice.

Henry flipped the reins with a sharp crack, and the curricle lurched forward as the horses began to run along even faster than before.

Nor did Henry let up the strenuous pace until they had come into a place that appeared to be more town than village.

"Ah," he sighed, bringing the horses to an easy halt as he stuck his head out and hailed a passing watchman.

"Good man, what is the hour?"

"It be half after eleven, your worthiness—"

At that moment a clock rang out the half hour.

"Aye, she be right on time. Ha'-past eleven it be, your worthiness."

"I take it we have reached Islington, have we not?"

"That ye have, your worthiness, an' if it be an inn ye wish, John Blarcom will take ye in. It be but a few—"

"Never mind, and thank you," replied Henry, tossing the man a copper. Then he urged on the horses, but at a more sober pace.

"The worst is over, my dear. We have less than three miles to traverse. In the daytime, it would be an hour's drive, what with all the traffic on the London streets, but we shall have it all to ourselves, and providing I do not lose our way, we should arrive with time to spare."

For the first time in what seemed hours to her, Ann was able to unclench her hands and sit back on the box.

"I am relieved to hear it, but I should venture to suggest that the worst is yet to come. How am I to carry myself before all those grand ladies?"

"I did not see that you had the least trouble at the Morgans' party. You know the respect due to rank, and you were never at a loss to say the right thing. Almack's will be no different."

"Indeed, my lord," said Ann, smiling to herself in the dark, "I must be honored that you should have taken such notice of me."

"It is nothing so remarkable. You put all of the other females in the shade. As a matter of fact, I feel perfectly justified in carrying out this business. You belong in Almack's, if that is any compliment to you."

"Thank you, my lord. You give me heart."

"Yes, but, as you mentioned, it is not to be all cakes and ale. You have got to remember who you are. You are Lady Horatia, sister to Viscount Blayde, and conduct yourself accordingly. Of course, it would not be a bad idea if you took some pains to avoid the Patronesses, although I pray you will not skulk about like a schoolgirl with a guilty secret."

"My lord, I shall do my best, but I beg of you never to desert my side. I am not your sister and, never having met her, I have not the faintest idea of her mannerisms."

"Yes, well, just not go to play-acting. If you will be yourself, as charming as you are beautiful, I do not think that there will be the least trouble— certainly not from the male attendees, I can assure you."

"Yes, it is the females I shall have to be on my

guard with. Oh, but I cannot believe that I shall not be found out the moment we step inside!"

"You forget, Ann, I shall be right beside you. It would be something difficult for anyone to contradict my presence with you. Surely I must know and be able to vouch for my own sister. No, upon that score, you have not a thing to worry about."

"I fervently pray you are right, my lord."

"If you insist upon calling me 'my lord,' I don't suppose I shall object, but Horatia does occasionally call me 'Henry.' It is not an unusual thing between brother and sister, you know."

Ann smiled: "Yes, Henry."

"Ah, that is quite better!" He reached out and patted her on the arm. "Rest assured, my dear, we shall pull it off."

"Perhaps. But there is the reckoning, tomorrow. I have still to face my father."

"Ann, my dear, it would be foolhardy in the extreme to let that thought spoil an exciting evening. We shall face Sir Joseph together on the morrow, and if it becomes necessary, I shall play the part of the villainous tempter. Never think on it until the time. I tell you it will all work itself out."

"Are you sure that your sister will not make an appearance tonight? I could never face her if she should."

Henry laughed. "That is the beauty of it. You have got her voucher. Without it, she knows she could never gain admittance, so even if she thought to attend, once she discovered her voucher was missing, she would have to give it up, you see. Of course, I suspect that she will have a few choice words to say to me after I disclose to her what use was made of it."

"Oh dear, she must be my enemy for life!" exclaimed Ann.

"She does not know you from Eve! No, her resentment, if any, will be directed to her beloved brother, who will be at pains to make up something in the nature of an excuse to satisfy her—well, perhaps I can mollify her at least. But this is poor stuff to be discussing at this point. See how far we have come! We are practically on the doorstep of Almack's. I pray you will put yourself in order so that we can make a fine appearance. I say, put on airs! You are a Vassall for the night. If you behave like one, no one will dare to question your right to be there!"

"There it is. Almack's!" remarked Henry, as the carriage rolled into James Street.

Suddenly Ann, who had been dozing a bit, was wide-awake. She leaned forward to stare over the horses at the building Henry had gestured at with his whip.

It was unmistakable in the night, but only for the brilliance of the golden light pouring from the first-story windows. It flickered with the passing of people back and forth in the Assembly Room and, as they drew near, the sound of a thousand voices raised in conversation reached out to them.

Ann's bosom heaved with excitement and her pulse raced rapidly. Her young life's ambition was about to be realized.

The curricle came to a stop before the undistinguished-looking glass doors and a man in livery came forth to take charge of the vehicle. While

Henry dismounted, the porter, dressed in silken breeches and hose, his hair powdered, so that he looked more a Duke attending a Royal Audience, assisted Ann out of the vehicle. He then waited for Henry to come to her and proceeded to lead the way to the entrance. There he stopped and turned.

Addressing Ann, he said, calmly: "May I have your voucher, your ladyship?"

In her excitement, Ann forgot that the precious bit of paper was in her hand and began to rummage through her reticule, growing more confused by the moment.

Gently, Henry caught her hand and extracted the voucher, saying, in a dry superior tone, and a smile: "It is my sister's first visit to the place, George."

The porter bowed stiffly, albeit with grace, stepped back, the voucher in his hand and opened the door.

"Lady Vassall, welcome to Almack's! If I may say so, your lordship, her ladyship will be an ornament to the Assembly."

"Thank you," said Ann, smiling sweetly at him.

"Ah, George, you always know what to say," said Henry with a laugh. "I do not know what the ladies would do without you."

He handed him a silver coin as Ann and he stepped within.

As they stood in the entrance hall, a furtive look came into Ann's eyes as she searched all about her for a familiar face, praying that she would not find one. Her wish was granted. Not only were all the people strangers to her, but there were so many of them, and she immediately felt more at ease.

In this crush, she was sure that she could remain unremarked for at least an hour.

Murmured Henry: "Do you see? There was nothing to it. In this crowd you are as safe as if you had never come. Now, I suggest that we do not stay in any one place too long, and I am sure you will pardon me if I avoid introducing you about. The less attention we attract, the easier it will be."

"Oh, but you will dance with me!" said Ann, looking up at him.

Henry, so much taller than she, was looking over the crowd. "It would not be the wisest thing to do. You see, you will be in everyone's sight out on the floor—"

He was interrupted by a gentleman approaching from the right. "I say, Blayde, never expected to see you here! And that is your sister? Oh, you devil! What an odious way to treat your friends! If the cat has got your tongue, it has not mine. Lady Horatia, had I the least hint as to what a beauty was the sister of this blackguard friend of mine, I should have parked myself upon the Vassall doorstep *sans* leave, *sans* invitation, until I had made your acquaintance. Since my bosom-beau has still to gather his wits about him, I shall dare to introduce me to you, myself. I have the honor to be Charles Fredrick Lord Tyrrell. My friends call me 'Freddie' and I should be delighted if you condescended to be my friend."

He said this with a bow, to which Ann responded with a curtsy, never leaving her hold on Henry's arm for an instant.

"What a delightful gentleman is your friend, Brother," she remarked, with a little simper.

Henry donned a rather insincere grin and nodded. He was about to pass some remark when Freddie rushed in to request: "My dear Horatia, you must put me down for your first dance. Henry, as merely your brother, can hardly object. I am sure he has some other lovely to squire."

He wheeled about and confronted Henry. "Do you have any idea of the hour? The dancing has been going on for some time and, like a fool, I signed every dance card I could get my hands on. Now, I must go to the trouble of explaining how family considerations demand that I excuse myself from my obligations so that I may do the proper with the daughter of the House of Vassall. Henry, just see the trouble you are putting me to."

"Look you, Freddie, it was a last minute decision. Until but a few hours ago, I had no thought that Horatia, or myself, would be setting foot in Almack's this night."

"Yes, I wondered about that. I do believe you mentioned how relieved you were that Horatia would be visiting in the country and you would not have the duty of her first appearance at Almack's. I say, Horatia, did you know Henry was such a curmudgeon?"

Ann replied: "Ah yes, you would be truly amazed at what we ladies are made to suffer at the hands of curmudgeonly brothers!"

"Come, let me take you away from him. The next dance is about to start, and if you do not join me on the dance floor, I suspect that you will be overwhelmed as soon as your attendance is remarked by the others, and I shall not get another chance."

"Yes, Horatia," said Henry. "I should like to

look about for a bit—to see if there is anyone about that we might know."

"But out on the floor, Henry? Did you not say—er...." She did not say more lest she say too much.

But Henry understood. "With you dancing, it might just flush out some of those very people we have *every* wish to meet. Freddie, have a care. She may be but my sister, but she is rather dear to me," he ended with a grin.

As he led Ann onto the floor, Freddie gave Henry an odd look.

"I say, what has come over your brother, Horatia? He seems to be a bit on the edge, don't you think?"

"Oh, I pray you will affect not to notice. Henry has no liking for having to squire his sister about; but he is a dear to have put his own wishes in the matter aside."

"But how the devil has he managed to keep you hidden from me all this time?"

"I dare say it is because we are far apart in age and Henry has his own establishment," replied Ann, her mind racing to anticipate Freddie's next question.

But the set had begun and she could be at ease on that score. It was a quadrille and the figures did not permit more than passing remarks.

The dance was concluded, and Freddie thanked her, but he could not stay for conversation. He was sure that he was in trouble with the partner whom he had skipped, and was in a hurry to find his next one before he would have too many excuses to make. In effect, he abandoned Ann to her own devices.

Once off the dance floor, a certain feeling of vulnerability descended upon her. Henry was not in sight, but that was only because she could not see over the crush. He could have been but a few steps away. In this crowded place, that small separation could compare with being at the ends of the earth, she was sure.

At any moment, someone might come along and discover that she was not the Horatia Vassall of past acquaintance, and she would have to face all the embarrassment of trying to explain the unexplainable by herself. Oh, where was Henry? She had felt so much safer upon the dance floor where no one could pounce upon her.

The edge of panic must have dulled her wits for she did hear someone say: "Lady Horatia? I beg your pardon, your ladyship."

It was not until the party cleared his throat and repeated himself that Ann came to with a start and turned quickly to face him.

It was the splendid porter who had taken her voucher up at the door. Her heart gave a leap of fright to see that in his hand he held a very similar paper. She looked into his face and was unable to read any expression there. She raised an unconscious hand to her throat and said: "Yes, I am Lady Horatia."

"Your ladyship, her ladyship, the Countess of Jersey, commands that you attend her in the sitting room. If you will please to follow your humble servant, I shall lead you to her ladyship."

He did not wait for her reply but turned about and started through the crowd, saying as he cleared a path for her: "I bid you make way, sir!

I bid you make way, your lordships," as they proceeded.

Ann had no choice but to follow him. The game was up and she was now about to receive her due. She had had the one dance, she had had her tiny fling in Almack's. The piper had played and now it was time to pay him. She did not think it had been worth it.

Every line of Lady Jersey's figure bespoke awareness of pride and authority. An empress might have envied her for her demeanor. She was sitting erect in a large and commodious chair as Ann came into the room, and her eyes rapidly measured the young lady without the least sign of approval.

Ann dropped into a curtsy and said: "My lady sent for me."

"Your manner is well enough. It is your behavior that is exceptional, Lady Horatia. I regret to say that we, the Patronesses of Almack's, require that you leave the premises."

Ann found that remark something of a puzzler. Since her ladyship was not calling her identity into account, her secret must not have been uncovered. Upon that score, she could feel easy—but what, in heaven's name, could the complaint against her be? She had had but the one dance, and she had not been about the place long enough to have stepped upon anyone's toes.

Lady Jersey was continuing: "Indeed, young lady, it pains me greatly to send you out. I shall have to make explanation to Lady Blayde, but I am sure she will agree that, at your very first appearance here, it was beyond propriety, it was insolent of you, to have ventured forth to dance without having secured our approval.

"My dear, I have known you from a child and—" At this point she applied a handsome, golden framed lorgnette to her eye and examined Ann once again.

"My, how the years do change us! Truly, my dear, you *have* changed. You were less than a schoolroom girl the last time I had a sight of you. Yes, it pleases me to say that you have grown into quite a handsome young lady—but you have something to learn, I fear, before you are ready for the rarefied heights of Almack's. I pray you return home and give thought to consideration and modesty. You have not enough of these qualities and I am sure that your mother, and your dear aunt, Lady Holland, will support me in this. Pray, who was it that brought you? I know that your parents are away." She frowned. "In fact I had the distinct impression that you would not be here this evening—"

Ann cut her off with: "It was my brother Henry, who escorted me. I humbly beg your forgiveness, my lady, but I quite agree that, having broken a rule, I should leave forthwith. If I am ever blessed with another voucher, I do assure you, I shall not be guilty of such a misstep again."

Lady Jersey's composure was shaken. "That is all you have to say? No protestations, no tears?"

At once Ann understood that she had made a slip. She ought to have been heartbroken. Instead, she had seen this eviction as the solution to her situation and not for anything did she wish to prolong the discomfort she had been suffering.

This was no way to come to Almack's and the sooner the ordeal was over and done with, the better.

"My lady, I am only trying to be sensible. Since I have merited your disapproval this evening, what is left for me to do is to regain it. I did not think that any histrionics on my part would swerve you from what you believe, and I believe, is your duty."

Lady Jersey sat and stared at her. "I do declare!" she breathed.

For a little while, there was silence in the room. Ann, impatient to be gone, suggested, at last: "If it is your ladyship's pleasure, I shall seek our Lord Blayde and explain to him what has occurred."

"That will not be necessary. I shall have him summoned and so inform him, myself—if *that* is what I decide to do. Lady Horatia, you are something different in a female than we are used to. You are old beyond your years."

Ann detected the note of indecision in Lady Jersey's tone and was engulfed by disappointment. It was beginning to appear that anything she said served only to embroil her more deeply. Was she never to escape?

The Countess was still staring at her, quite unable to make up her mind. Her face was cast in an expression of disapproval and her hands were clasped in her lap.

For Ann, the suspense was nigh unbearable. She had the feeling that the longer she remained in Almack's, the worse things would get. Somehow she had got to extricate herself from this room and the establishment before a greater doom befell her. Oh, if only Henry had been at her side!

"No!" said Lady Jersey, at last. "No, I regret to say that there can be no exceptions made. Were I to make allowance for you, my dear Horatia, I have no doubt but that we should be deluged with all manner of misbehavior and, what is worse, gross infractions of our rules. While I admire your demeanor at this pass, all that I can promise is that next Season, we shall give due consideration to you. In the meantime, I must insist that you depart the premises at once. I shall send for Lord Blayde immediately."

She was about to give a tug to the bellrope when there was a light knock on the door and Lady Cowper came into the room.

She was looking quite beautiful, her glossy dark hair a marvelous contrast to her fair complexion and red, full lips. She was smiling brightly as she gushed: "Ah, Sarah, there you are! I have been looking all over for you!"

"Emily!" exclaimed Lady Jersey, rising to clasp hands with her. "I am sure we never expected you! What a delightful surprise!"

Ann, her heart in her mouth, quickly got out of her chair, dipped in a slight curtsy and stepped to the door, praying to escape before Lady Emily recognized her.

"Lady Horatia, I did not give you leave to depart!" said Countess Jersey. "Come and allow me to present you to the Countess of Cowper."

It was all up with Ann. The worst that could happen was about to befall her. Even as she stepped forth, Lady Cowper exclaimed: "Ann Keating, what on earth are you doing here?"

With a superior smile, Lady Jersey intervened. "My dear Emily, I fear you are suffering under a misapprehension. This is Horatia Vassall. You, who are so thick with the Hollands and the Vassalls, surely must recall the daughter of the house. Step forth, Horatia. Lady Cowper will not bite you."

Ann did as she was bid, a stricken look in her eyes, not daring to look up at Lady Cowper, who stood staring at her aghast.

Lady Jersey continued. "We have here what is a most difficult case, Emily. This young lady dared to join in the dance without permission, and this is her first attendance at our Assembly. I had no choice but to dismiss her from the festivities for the remainder of the Season. Since I it was who sponsored her, I am sure that the other ladies of the board will not take exception. Of course, we shall have to reconsider Horatia's standing for the following Season."

By this time, a sour smile wreathed Lady Cowper's lips. "Sarah, surely, you are joking. Oh, surely you have not let yourself be taken in by this imposter!"

Lady Jersey turned upon the Countess of Cowper and demanded: "Whatever do you mean?"

"Now do you see what comes of your tendering vouchers to candidates, sight unseen? Here you have got a brash young upstart, an Ann Keating, not an Horatia Vassall—"

"Emily, I fear you are gone quite dotty. I am sure I know the Vassalls very well indeed, and what need have I for any further proof of the young lady's identity than her voucher *and* the fact of her having been brought here by her very own brother. Do you question the word of Henry Vassall with regard to the identity of his own sister?"

"Sarah, you have been made a fool of, my word upon it. Speak up, young lady! Who are you!"

"As your ladyship knows, I am Ann Keating," said Ann, in a very small voice, and immediately fell aweeping.

Lady Jersey's eyes opened wide with astonishment. She gasped: "Never in my life have I been so shocked! Horrors! How could she have managed? I thought we had taken every precaution to avoid just such a situation. Emily, what are we to do? Do you realize what this will do to our reputation? How foolish we shall be made to look? Who *is* this person? I demand to know? Keating? Keating? The name does have a familiar ring— Ah!" and she shot an accusing eye at Lady Cowper.

Ann was completely ignored as Lady Cowper began to look uncomfortable.

"Yes!" exclaimed Lady Jersey. "I recall it now. This is the very person you insisted, despite her lack of station, despite her lack of breeding, as we now see very clearly—this is the person you would have tendered a voucher to. At our very next meeting, Emily, I shall bring charges against you before our sister Patronesses, for putting a stain upon our reputation—"

Lady Cowper turned upon Ann: "Oh, you ungrateful girl! Do you see what you have done? Had you no patience? Here in my purse is the very voucher that would have admitted you to Almack's without the least fuss. But no, you had to take matters into your own hands and ruin everything. Miss Keating, I demand to know how you came into possession of the voucher intended for Lady Horatia Vassall!"

"Indeed!" exclaimed Lady Jersey. "If I can believe my ears, this young person, masquerading as a lady, must be given in charge to the authorities. Now that I look at her, I am shocked at my lack of discernment. We have got us a thief in our midst! A veritable area-snitch, I believe the word is!"

"Sarah, I pray you to compose yourself!" snapped Lady Cowper. "This is no time for hyperbole. I shall vouch for the fact that Miss Keating is indeed a gentlewoman—and it is not area-snitch but area-sneak, my dear, which, incidentally, is of the opposite sex—"

"I am sure I am beholden to you, my dear, for this bit of erudition, but it does not change the face of the matter. The girl is, quite obviously, beyond redemption and must be handed over to the authorities. As for our little society, here at Almack's, I am distraught to think of what will be said once it is learned that a base person gained entrance to Almack's under the most false of pretenses—"

"Sarah, if you intend to go on in that hysterical fashion, truly, all that you are prophesying will come to pass! It is going to take calm thinking and collected consideration, if we are to work ourselves out of this mess," Lady Cowper pointed out.

"If you have something to suggest, Emily, then you must speak up. Of course, I cannot promise that charges will not be brought against you for bringing to jeopardy the fair flower of England's most exclusive people—"

Lady Cowper, with a look of disgust, turned away from Lady Jersey and addressed Ann: "Tears are not the answer, Miss Keating. I think that we all must put our heads together and talk out this business. Do be seated, young lady, and you, too, Sarah. I pray that none of you have any other obligations this evening. If you do, speak up, so that appropriate messages can be sent and excuses made. Not a one of us is to stir one foot outside this room until we have settled things!"

"Emily Cowper, I am quite sure that if there is anything to be done in this matter, I shall have the doing of it!" declared Lady Jersey, sternly. "I suggest that not only am I the president of the Ladies of Almack's, but there are a few Earls that Lord Jersey follows in the line of precedence."

"Sarah, this is no time to compare dignities— ah, but if that is what you will have, be damned to Almack's! I shall let you watch our little society sink into the sea of disgrace, overwhelmed by the malicious tongues that even now are wagging to no complimentary purpose—"

"Oh, Emily, there is no need to go all over touchy! Of course, if you have got any sort of solution that will rectify this disgrace, whilst it metes out an appropriate chastisement to this young miscreant—"

"You had better make up your mind, here and now, Sarah. Which is the more important, the reputation of Almack's or this girl's punishment? You cannot have it both ways. If you would save Almack's, you must save Miss Keating. The one is tied to the other."

Ann had ceased to weep for some time now. The exchange between the two Countesses had put all thought of her own trouble aside. She could not imagine what the difficulty was. She had been caught red-handed, as it were, and could offer no acceptable excuse for her misbehavior. At the beginning, she had been resigned to the fact that the bitter dregs of disgrace were to be her portion for the rest of her life, so that not even a place as far from London as was Cheltenham could serve to ameliorate her fall in any degree. Yet, from what she was hearing, there was a chance, there was hope, that what would ensue would not be all *that* bad for her. It was impossible to maintain her disconsolation in the face of Lady Cowper's surprising attitude.

A number of times she had wished to interject a remark in her own defense, to inform Lady Jersey how thoroughly ashamed she was of herself, how deeply she regretted, now that it was too late, the awful thing she had done; but, it seemed to her, Lady Cowper's odd tack was not to be interfered with. Time enough to cast herself upon their ladyships' respective mercies after the dust had settled a bit.

"...You see, Emily, she is not even paying the least attention to us!" Lady Jersey was saying. "Oh, callous girl! Oh, how you make us suffer!"

By this time, Lady Cowper was looking quite nettled. Her friend and colleague was quite unable to master her indignation, with the result that the discussion was completely stalled.

She got up from her chair and came to stand before Lady Jersey.

"Now look you, Sarah, we are not—"

At that moment there was a knock on the door of the small room and the porter put in his head.

"I beg your pardon, your ladyships, but there is a gentleman outside inquiring as to the whereabouts of the young lady."

With an august air, Lady Jersey informed the

fellow that under no circumstances were they to be disturbed.

"Just a moment, my good man! Who is the gentleman?" asked Lady Cowper.

"Lord Blayde an it please you, your ladyship."

"It makes no difference were he Prince George—" began Lady Jersey, but Lady Cowper had seen the look in Ann's eyes at the mention of Henry's name.

"On the contrary, that is precisely the gentleman we wish to see. I beg your pardon, Sarah, but I have more than a suspicion that Henry can throw some light on this mess—and, furthermore, we shall have need of him to assist us in what we needs must do. Show him in!"

"But, Emily, it is just one more mouth to spread it about—"

"I think not. I think Henry is involved and him we can manage by making an appeal to Lady Holland."

"That woman? I have no wish to speak to her, much less appeal to her. She has not deigned to join us and it gives me to believe that she has no great thought for the important work we do here."

"Nonetheless, if there is to be a blot upon the Holland family, I venture to say that she will wish to be informed. I know for a fact that Henry and Miss Keating are acquainted."

"Oh, Emily, if that scapegrace had had a hand in the business, then are we done for!" she wailed.

"Did I hear someone mention me in sweet compliment?" inquired Henry, coming into the room with a saucy grin on his face.

"Oh, you dear boy!" exclaimed Countess Jersey.

"You have been quite naughty! Why did you not come to me and let me know you were here?"

"I was rather occupied— Oh dear!" he exclaimed as his glance encountered Ann's unhappy countenance. "Ann, are you all right?"

"Aha! It is just as I thought! Emily, we are ruined!" Lady Jersey declared, making the statement as though it was an uncontradictable fact.

CHAPTER 11

"Henry Vassall, if you have had a hand in this monstrous affair, you have much to answer for," declared Lady Cowper.

Henry disregarded her and went over to Ann. "How did it happen?" he asked. "I was sure that we had taken all precautions."

"It is quite obvious that we had not," returned Ann, coldly.

Henry wheeled about and said accusingly to Lady Cowper: "Emily, it is all your fault. I'll take my oath that we would not have been discovered, but that you came upon the scene and it was all up with us. I was sure you would not be attending this Assembly. Emily, why did you change your mind? We could have pulled it off to perfection if you had not."

"Really, Henry, that is quite bad of you! Are

you so weak that a pretty face is all that is necessary to bring you to behave in the most outrageous fashion? You know I shall have to lay this before your aunt, Lady Holland, do you not?"

Henry smiled a sour smile. "It is not Aunt Bess that troubles me, but Horatia. She is under the impression that her voucher is safely ensconced in her bureau drawer. I suspect that she will have a thing or two to say to me."

"Well, young man, we have a thing or two to say to you, this very moment!" declared Lady Jersey. "Of course, as you are a male, it is to be expected a person, such as we have here, can lead you by the nose if she is so disposed—"

"Sarah, you do me an injustice! The entire idea was mine, and I think it was quite clever of me to have carried it out—"

"I assure you, dear boy, it never would have succeeded, the girl has not the faintest idea of the behavior required in a superior society. It was I who caught her out—"

He turned to Ann. "Is this true? I was sure you had the presence to fit in here."

"It was the dancing, Henry. I had no idea that permission to dance was required—"

He clapped his hand to his head. "Blast! Then it was my fault! I ought to have remembered that little bit of nonsense. Only Sarah would have made such an issue of it. But, I say, it would appear that she did not tumble to the fact that you were not Horatia."

"True. It was Lady Cowper who caught me out as soon as she laid eyes upon me. Oh, Henry, what am I to do? Her ladyship would bring charges against me."

"Don't be silly! Since this little frolic is fraught with the most scandalous implications which are bound to reflect on Almack's, no one is about to air the dirty linen in public."

"How very uncouth of you!" commented Lady Jersey.

"How very wise of me, my lady. I did take this possibility into account, you see. This is the worst that could have happened. Unfortunately it did and so we must decide what is to be done. As I see it, none of us wishes the matter to go beyond these doors."

"But I do not understand *your* purpose in all of this, sir!" said Lady Cowper, sternly. "What did you have to gain by it?"

Henry's smile flashed out. "It appeared a bit of a rum go, don't you know. Here was this lovely young thing, pining away for a glimpse into this glorious interior, and there was I with not a thing to do. And, besides, there was a bit of a challenge in it. You must admit that if it had not been for you, my lady, we should have put it over, quite."

"He is not in the least repentant!" exclaimed Lady Jersey. "His aunt shall hear of this, my oath upon it!"

She turned to reexamine Ann. "Hmph!" she gave a little snort of disdain. "They are both of them cut out of the same cloth!"

It was more than enough for Ann. "Oh no, your ladyship," she protested, "I pray you will believe me that I am indeed deeply remorseful. For this one short experience of Almack's, I have fairly lost my reputation. Indeed, nothing is worth so high a price, certainly not Almack's."

"Well, I do declare!" exclaimed Lady Jersey.

"Will you listen to the creature, Emily? Now it would appear that *we* are not good enough for *her*. I swear I do not know what the world would come to if it were not for you and I and others like us, dignified, respectable people who make it a matter of pride to preserve the old, refined elegance that has become so rare these days and just because of people like her. How you could ever have contemplated conferring a voucher upon this one, I do not know."

"Oh, Sarah, I do wish you had not mentioned that!" exclaimed Lady Emily, casting a wary eye at Henry.

"What is this I hear? Emily, you were actually about to admit this lovely young girl to the collective bosoms of Almack's? Then what in Old Harry's name is this all about?"

"Do you see, Sarah, what you have done? Henry is not about to let *that* opportunity escape him," pointed out Lady Cowper. "Now, we are on less firm ground than we had been."

"Good heavens, Henry," rejoined Lady Jersey. "You are not going to allow that misguided consideration to lessen the crime? Miss Keating had no knowledge of Emily's benevolence. She invaded our premises in cold blood—"

"Ah, but that was only because the ride down was rather cool, you see," he replied with a laugh.

Her ladyship was quite offended at his levity and tossed her chin at him, not deigning to respond to his impudence.

Lady Cowper sighed. "Oh, Ann, what are we going to do about you?"

Ann was looking very contrite. "My lady, it is all up with me. All is lost, and I tremble with pain at the thought that Sir Joseph must be made aware of it."

"Shut up, you little imbecile! The game is far from over!" snapped Henry. "I am not about to sit idly by and allow these two to make a hash of *my* reputation! I am considered a bit of a scapegrace already; I am not about to stand still for my name becoming synonymous for 'cad' and 'blackguard.'"

He turned to Emily. "Now there *is* something that has escaped our consideration. Sir Joseph is not a well man and this news is bound to cause him something of a setback. We must take all pains to avoid it."

"You ought to have thought of that before you began this horrid trickery!" she retorted.

"I tell you, it is not too late. All you and Sarah have got to do is to keep your mouths shut about the business— I shall take care of Horatia upon that score, if it is at all necessary—whilst I carry Ann back to Hertfordshire this very night. My horses are well rested and I can have her back in her house before the sun rises, my word upon it."

"Henry, are you out of your skull?" exclaimed Lady Cowper. "That would make matters only worse than they are! Imagine what would be said, you and she alone together all night and until the wee hours of the morning. Not on your life, my boy! She has got to stay with me in London."

"Hm, that sounds very promising. Still, how did she manage to get to you? Sir Joseph has *got* to ask that question."

Lady Cowper was rubbing her eyebrow with one hand, looking troubled. "Yes, that explains nothing. What do you suggest to explain it?"

Lady Jersey intervened. "I think this conversation is disgraceful! That it should actually be taking place while an Assembly, the finest and most elegant Assembly in all of England, is going on, is too shocking to be borne. Emily, you are not condoning what these two have done, are you? For, if you are, you may count me out of it! I shall not rest until this person, this Miss Keating, receives her just deserts."

"Sarah, I do believe that there are times when one must stand up for what is proper. This, my dear, is *not* one of them. I admit I do not care to see Miss Keating get off scot-free, but I should like it even less if, because of her, all that we have worked for were to go up in the smoke of gossip, a fire which will incinerate Almack's and all we have tried to do. Sarah, you have got to consider all the aspects of what we propose to do. We are sitting in judgment upon the fate of English society. It is as much as you have always pointed out to the rest of us, the sacred role that Almack's plays in modern England."

To Ann that was a silly appeal and she waited for Lady Jersey's scornful rejection. It did not come. Her ladyship was seriously considering the point, and much to Ann's surprise, nodded a reluctant assent.

Ann's eyes opened wide with surprise as Lady Cowper picked up her purse, and from it, took out a very familiar-looking bit of paper.

"Here, Ann, you do not deserve it, but it goes to make your presence here licit."

"For me?" Ann asked, unbelieving, fearing to take the voucher from her ladyship.

"Oh, do not make such a fuss about it, girl!" Lady Jersey remarked, angrily. "You have us on the hip, as the saying goes. If you dare to crow about it, nothing, nothing in God's universe will stop me from revoking it!"

"Yes, your ladyship. Thank you, your ladyships. It is my dream come true."

"Hah!" exclaimed Henry. "I dare say that settles that."

"Not so fast, dear boy. There is lots more to be done," said Lady Cowper. "We have quite talked the night away. I am sure I hear the very last set being played and we still are nowhere as far as the further disposition of Ann is concerned."

"Well, I am sure that is no concern of mine," he replied, airily. "Now, I have got to be going—"

"Indeed you do!" retorted Lady Cowper. "You have a ride before you—back to Hertfordshire, to inform Sir Joseph as to the whereabouts of his daughter."

"Come now, Emily, you are carrying things too far! With that bit of paper in her hand, everything is done up quite neatly. She is here under your approval; you have got yourself a guest and nothing more be said about it. Sir Joseph can hardly look askance at his daughter's attending an Assembly. I dare say it will be rather pleasant news to him when he receives it, but nothing about which he has to take exception."

"You idiot! It is his approval that is needed to patch things over!"

"But it is already done! Even if he should disapprove—although I cannot imagine him doing such a thing—the deed is done."

"Have you no sense? He has got to be informed so that he can put a good face upon it. You have got to go out to him, explain things any way you wish, but making sure that he understands the situation. Then, whatever the gossips may report, he can meet them with the rebuttal that he had given his approval to the entire business. He would have carried Ann to London himself had his health permitted it. Instead, you were selected for the honor, because you are a gentleman of the first degree and could be trusted with such a precious charge."

"Oh, I say! I shall be all blushing in a moment if you continue to say such sweet things of me," he retorted with a grin.

Her ladyship smiled and added: "That is how it has to be. Had I any notice of the facts, *you,* my sweet prince, would have been the last man on earth I should have trusted with Ann."

Ann did not think that remark a fair one. "My lady," she said, "I must protest. Lord Blayde was most obliging and, in the highest degree, proper throughout our journey. I should trust myself with him at any time and in any place."

Henry bowed low to her. Lady Jersey exclaimed: "Tommyrot!" and Lady Cowper smiled wryly.

"Yes," said the latter, "that is what is bedeviling me. Henry, is it at all possible that you have turned over a new leaf?"

He laughed. "Oh, I am not such a bad fellow when all is said and done."

"I am so relieved to hear it. Then you will make no further objections and get cracking back to Sir Joseph with the explanations that are due him."

Henry sighed. "I will admit that I did not forsee *this* denouement. Are you quite sure that Ann could not go back with me? I mean to say, as long as none of us are going to open our mouths about the business, she could be back in Hertfordshire and no one the wiser for her absence."

Said Ann: "No, Henry, it is not possible. The Morgans and the rest of our neighbors must be aware by this time that I am gone, and they will certainly think to inform Sir Joseph of my disappearance. I have had a taste of your driving, and I imagine that you will have to go like the wind. Truly, I am not up to a second course over the roads."

Henry drew a long face. "I had thought that my company might have been a sufficient attraction—but, if that is how you feel about it, I shall have to go it alone. Ladies, I bid you all a fond farewell."

He bowed to them and strode out of the room.

Mused Ann: "Actually, I should have liked to return with him."

"Oh? Then why did you not? I could not have kept you if you wished to," said Lady Cowper.

"Obviously, the girl is not witless," said Lady Jersey. "She does not really believe Henry Vassall is all *that* trustworthy."

Ann drew herself up and replied: "That is not true, your ladyship. I do trust Henry. It is myself I do not trust—with him," she added, quickly.

Lady Emily laughed.

CHAPTER 12

As a greatly fatigued Viscount Blayde drew rein before the modest structure of the Keatings in Tewin, the dawn was beginning to fill the air with a dreamy half light that only added strain to his weary eyes. He was relieved to have come to the end of his journey, but very loath to descend from his seat in the curricle. His horses, too, showed no spirit as they moved their foam-flecked heads about and dropped them abruptly.

At that early hour, there was no one to take charge of his beasts and his vehicle. In fact, now that he had arrived, he was not sure that he was about to do the right thing, rousing the household for the purpose of presenting to Sir Joseph that which, in the dawn's cold light, begged more of an explanation than he cared to supply. Now that the effort of finding his way at a smart pace through the dark roads of Hertfordshire was done with, and he could devote his mind to his errand, he began to see what appeared most reasonable amidst the glitter of St. James Street was, in Tewin, not likely to be easily swallowed, nor to be received with approval.

With a sigh, he descended from his dusty carriage and, acting his own groom, led the beasts around to the rear of the house where he thought to find an accommodation for them. He had not progressed far along the gravel walk when someone unshuttered a dark lantern in his face, blinding him.

"Stand and deliver!" a voice rang out.

Henry let out a curse. Of all places to encounter a highwayman, he thought. He came to a stop and raised one hand.

The lantern-holder drew closer and demanded: "Who the devil are you and what are you doing on these premises?"

"I might request the same information of you, my good man. If you are training a pistol upon me, I assure you I am unarmed. My purse is in my breast pocket and you may have it and its entire contents, only go away and do not bother me."

"How dare you insult me! Do you take me for a footpad?"

"Are you not?" asked Henry in surprise. "You have come to rob me, haven't you?"

"Sir, whoever you are, I shall send my seconds to meet with yours on the morrow! No man can insult me and live to repeat the offense!"

"If you are not what I believe you to be, why do you demand that I 'stand and deliver'? That is precisely what a highwayman says to his victims."

"I beg your pardon, but it was the only thing I could think of at the moment," said the voice, lamely. "I am not exactly sure of what one does say to a prowler. I say, do you know?"

"I have the feeling that I have to deal with an idiot. Put that blasted lantern down! You are quite blinding me."

"I beg your pardon, sir," he said as he lowered the lantern.

Now Henry could make out a young man, completely unarmed, well dressed, and not uncomely. He was almost as tall as the Viscount.

Said Henry: "I demand to know, sir, what business you have got sneaking about the residence of Sir Joseph Keating. I warn you to speak the truth, for I see you are unarmed and never a match for me if it comes to a mill between us."

"I assure you, sir, I have every right to be concerned with the visit of an unknown gentleman who appears to be taking liberties with my father's domicile."

"Ah-h!" said Henry, with great relief. "Then I take it you are brother to Ann."

"Who the devil are you, sir, to make use of my sister's name so freely? I insist upon an answer."

"I am Henry, Viscount Blayde, and who may you be?"

"I am Christopher Keating, only son and heir to Sir Joseph Keating, Bart."

"I am intimately acquainted with your father, Christopher. In fact, that is why I am come, directly out of London, to satisfy the gentleman as to the safety and well-being of his daughter."

"Ann? *You* know about Ann? Lord Blayde, I am not sure I care for your manner. You appear to affect an innocence that does not gibe with the circumstances. I have just come down from Oxford—that is, I have just been sent down—"

Henry grinned. "I take it that you engaged in something more than your curriculum called for?"

Christopher waved it aside with his hand. "It is nothing. I thought I had got inside the wall without having been noticed, but the Proctor was sharper than I thought— But that is not to the point, my lord. I came home to find my poor father, who should have been taking his rest, awake at a late hour, filled with worry for the safety of his daughter, my sister. You, sir, claim to have knowledge of her whereabouts, which is not at all encouraging. I was about to ride out to the Morgans', where I hoped to gain word of her. You see, they were giving a party—"

"Yes, yes, I know all about it. As a matter of fact, I was there and—"

"Then, if you have any heart in you at all, you must come within at once, instead of skulking about, and relieve the anxiety of an old man who is not well—"

"Imbecile!" snapped Henry. "What do you think I rode all through the night to reach this place if it was not precisely for that reason! I have come to inform Sir Joseph that his daughter is quite safe—"

"Ah, I see what it is? You have kidnapped Ann, and have come to present my father with a demand for her ransom—"

Henry, filled to the full with exasperation and weariness, could bear the conversation no longer. He reached out and grabbed Christopher by his neckband and pulled him close. Snarling in his face, he growled: "My young gentleman, but recently sent down from Oxford, hear me and hear me well! I am excessively weary and more than short-tempered. Take me to your father at once, and cease this childish idiocy. Blast your hide, Ann is safer at this moment than she could ever be. There is no plot— But there is an urgent requirement that I inform Sir Joseph of what has occurred. Now stow your gab and pike it!"

Although he was much shaken, Christopher tore himself free from Henry's grasp and said: "It had better be a good tale you have for us, my lord, or you shall have to answer to me! This way, if you please. My father has not slept a wink this night and you will find him in the drawing room. Have a care, sir, for he is not a well man."

As Henry followed Christopher into the house, he said: "It is quite all right. I know Sir Joseph and am acquainted with his condition. I shall take every care to reassure him."

Upon their entrance into the tiny drawing room, Sir Joseph, his face drawn and haggard from a sleepless night of tension, arose, and his face broke into a smile of recognition.

"My Lord Blayde! What a pleasure to renew my acquaintance with you! Then you have brought Ann back to me? Where is she? I have been half out of my mind with worry—"

"I beg your pardon, Sir Joseph; although Ann is quite safe, she is not with me. At this moment, she is enjoying the hospitality of Lady Cowper in her London residence. You see—"

"Dad, his lordship strikes me as being a smooth 'un. I should not trust him," put in Christopher.

"In fact, I discovered him prowling about the premises. I insisted he come inside and speak with you. I should go on to the Morgans', but I did not think it wise to leave him alone with you."

Sir Joseph looked puzzled and stared a question at Henry. "I do not think I quite understand any of this, my lord," he said.

"I fear that your scion has got things rather twisted about, Sir Joseph. Actually, I have just ridden all the way up from London to present you with a narrative of what has transpired this evening. I admit, at the outset, that my actions in the matter were not of the most circumspect, but—"

"Oh, he is smooth, he is!" declared Christopher. "See how he puts off telling you about Ann."

"Christopher, it will be years yet before I am so enfeebled that I shall have to rely upon a son who has been sent down from Oxford. You, sir, are the last one whose conversation is required in this instance. Now, I demand you make your apologies to Lord Blayde and, henceforth, hold your tongue. I shall have a few words to say to you with regard to your misbehavior at Oxford. I bid you think upon *that!*"

Christopher mumbled an apology and retired to the side of the room. His father turned to Henry and said: "Now then, my lord, I am patiently awaiting what it is you have to tell me about Ann. To say I am worried for her welfare is to put it mildly indeed."

Henry immediately prefaced his narrative with assurances that there was truly nothing to worry about. Nothing had befallen Ann but what was good. Then he went off into his story, not sparing any detail. He did not see that it would be the least profitable to withhold anything from Sir Joseph—and, besides, he was much too weary to take the pains of fabricating something more acceptable.

When he had done, he paused and regarded Sir Joseph.

The Baronet was silent for a time, his gaze upon Henry, his lips pursed, and his eyes narrowed in anger. Finally, he said, very coldly: "Sir, you are no gentleman. That it has turned out as well as it has is no credit to you. I am beholden to the Countess of Cowper for her mercy. After this odious business is settled, I must bid you never to see my daughter again."

"Oh, I say, Sir Joseph, there never was any great risk—"

"That there was any risk at all to a fine young lady ought to have been sufficient cause to have put this scandalous elopement out of your mind, sir!" he said, sternly. "Now then, from what you have said, there are still things to do. I am grateful to you, of course, for your not abandoning Ann, and, of course, you will assent to carrying me to London, at once, so that I may see and speak with my daughter and with her ladyship, Countess Cowper. After that, we shall return to Tewin, and I shall make a point of calling upon Mrs. Morgan to make whatever apologies appear to be called for—"

"Good heavens, you are not about to inform her of what happened—"

"Of course not, your lordship. But the woman has to be told something. Only after I have conferred with Lady Cowper shall I know precisely what to say. Obviously, we must make sure that all our stories march along with each other."

"Quite. Then I shall retire to Panshanger for a day's rest and come for you tomorrow—"

"Not a bit, your lordship! You will take me to Ann at once. I shall not brook the slightest delay!"

"Oh, I beg you to be merciful, Sir Joseph! I have been up driving all the night. You can not expect it of me! A half-day's rest is all I require—"

"And I, sir, require to speak with my daughter! You have transgressed against me and mine. You are under obligation, sir, to see that all is settled as quickly as is possible."

"Very well, Sir Joseph, we go to London upon the instant. Heaven preserve my poor beasts!"

"We can start with a pair of mine and change at the inns when necessary."

Said Christopher: "I pray that you will allow me to accompany you, Father."

"Yes, that would be a very good idea. It will be a lesson to you, my son, how rash, inconsiderate conduct on the part of one member can plunge an entire family into the depths of misery and despair."

"But Ann has got herself a voucher to Almack's," protested Christopher.

Sir Joseph threw up his hands in disgust. "That is all you young people ever think of: What has been gained; never what has been lost!"

"But we have lost nothing that I can see."

"Does not Ann's good name mean anything to you? Sometimes I think it is a sheer waste to raise up children! They have no idea of consequences!"

The three gentlemen who emerged from the carriage that drew up before the Cowpers' London town house in the vicinity of nine o'clock the next morning were something the worse for their nocturnal journey. All of them showed signs of having missed their sleep. Lord Blayde was staggering as he came around to assist Sir Joseph to descend. His face was worn and haggard, and his eyes were dark and sunken.

Sir Joseph showed more the strain of the ride than fatigue, although he was anything but fresh.

Christopher, of the three, was the brightest in appearance; his clothes however showed wear and tear beyond the usual. His coat was a piece with the canopy of the curricle which, too, displayed a gaping hole or two, the marks made by vicious brambles in resentment of a carriage that came blundering off the road into their domain. Obviously, it had been a poor showing by Henry because of his excessive fatigue, the occasional loss of control and mastery of the road that had beset him during the drive.

The footman, who answered the door, frowned in protest at the unshaven, travel-stained strangers that requested admittance to Lord and Lady Cowper. It was only that he managed to recognize Viscount Blayde that he did not slam the door in their faces.

He quickly recovered himself and led the gentlemen to a small study to wait while he went to inform his mistress of their presence.

As Sir Joseph settled himself into an easy chair with a tenderness that suggested his unwillingness to disturb his aching body any more than was necessary, he gasped: "My lord, I do not think that I could survive another such night with you at the reins."

Henry, who was trying to rub the weariness out of his eyes with both fists, nodded: "I quite agree with you, sir. Another such night of perilous driving and I should swear off the ribbons forever. I still do not think it was all that necessary."

He looked at Christopher who was grinning at him and demanded: "What do you find that is so funny, whelp?"

"It was a smashing go, my lord! Despite the cost to my clothing, I would jump at the chance to do it again, but with myself at the reins. You made excellent time, but I am sure I could have done it faster."

Henry merely groaned and turned his head away.

CHAPTER 13

The sound in the street brought Ann awake with a start. It was a sound which she had not heard since childhood when the City claimed her as a resident.

Over and over again the cry was repeated, swelling in volume as the costermonger came down the street and dying away as he passed by: "Hullo! Hullo here! beautiful lobsters! good and cheap! fine cock crabs all alive O!"

She smiled at the nostalgic twinge she felt and got up out of bed.

As she looked about her, through the bed-curtains, at the beautiful and expensive appointments of this guest bedroom of the Cowpers, she marveled that she should find herself here. Last night had been a time of great fear, alternating with waves of relief, as the consequences of her mad escapade with Henry brought condemnation, which was justified, and promises of escape from disgrace, which was not justified. As a result, this morning she was filled with a strong sense of guilt upon arising.

Actually she was not quite sure what her status in the Cowper household was. Was she prisoner or was she guest? She did not know.

Not that it made any difference. Sir Joseph was bound to be extremely disappointed in her and his condemnation was what she truly feared, and expected.

Lady Cowper had given every appearance, upon carrying her home from Almack's, of having an unwelcome guest upon her hands, and had sent her right off to bed in the company of a maidservant. Ann had been just as glad to be relieved of having to maintain a polite acceptance of Lady Cowper's unhappiness with her. The business did not bear discussing. Until her father had been informed, nothing much could be done with her.

There was nothing comforting in the thought. As poorly as she might feel about the affair, as truly regretful as she might express herself, the die of her disgrace was cast, and from this moment forward, she could never meet the world on those pleasant terms that she had enjoyed in the past. No, even Sir Joseph must, in the future, always view his daughter with a doubting look he could never disguise.

And then there was Henry! Oh, what a scapegrace he was! If it had not been for him, none of this would have taken place!

Although she might be the last person in the world, at this stage, to be able to condemn anyone, he she could condemn. It had been all his fault in every way!

No, it hadn't, she thought. Not really. There was no part of the blame she could escape by passing it off onto his shoulders. She had been willing, more than willing, in the final analysis, to succumb to his temptation. His glib assurances that they should never be discovered were in gross contradiction to what her own good sense had counseled, and *she* had ignored it. It was never a case of she should have known better, for she had known better and yet had joined Henry without a qualm, relying upon his glibness that all would be successful.

Oh, he was a one that no young lady should have to put up with! It was not fair of her to put all the blame on him, she knew, but she could not help her feelings in the matter. He had insinuated himself into her life and all had changed for the worse. She could never express the fullness of her regret at having made his acquaintance.

But Ann had no tears for herself. She knew the tally quite well. From now on, people would expect the worst of her; they would say to each other out of the side of their mouths, with knowing leers: "She is no better than she should be!" It was to be her fate and nothing would change it.

Fortunately, as the matter did concern the good name of the Patronesses of Almack's, she would not be made to suffer the fate of the outcast. She must needs be tolerated to preserve the fair reputation of that bastion of the English *beau monde,* namely, Almack's. In that one regard, Henry had planned it well.

She had been amazed at his impudent manner

before the two Countesses. And even more, she had been floored to see how they had come about and finally agreed that her fate was of minor consequence as compared to what might be thought of Almack's exclusiveness.

Before that had come clear, she had had visions of being forced to live out the rest of her days in some shepherd's cot, a spinster forever, pining away in the northern wilds of Cumberland where polite society need never again give thought to her. For Henry, she could spare some gratitude. Such an odious consequence of her misbehavior was not to be. Confined, she might be; that would be up to her father to decide. But the chance of it all blowing over was now much improved and a prospect of some reasonable sort of existence was quite favorable.

Ann concluded that there was no point in kicking against fate. It would not be as bad as it might have been. Her best way was to accept whatever was meted out to her with utter resignation and pray that the odious business would fade to nothing in the memory of those who came to know of it.

Her resignation was so complete that her languid tug on the bellrope for a maid was ineffective and she had to repeat it with some firmness.

She was in the midst of her toilet when the door to her chamber suddenly opened. At once the thought leaped into her mind: She *was* a prisoner!

Without a knock or a by-your-leave, Lady Cowper entered and began to address her.

"Ah, it is good to see that you have arisen, young lady! I did not think you could have slept all that well after what we have been through. Please to ready yourself as quickly as possible. Your father has come and awaits you."

Ann's resignation proved incomplete. She was about to face her father and she was suddenly all atremble.

"Th-thank you, your ladyship," she faltered. Then she took a deep breath, dismissed her maid, and stepped forward.

Holding herself stiffly erect, she thrust out her chin, and declared in a voice strained and quavering: "I am ready!"

The expression on Lady Cowper's face softened. There was a slight smile on her lips as she replied: "Indeed, I am sure that Mary, Queen of Scots, could not have done it better. My dear, I assure you it was never in my mind to see you trampled in the dust and, with the help of Henry Vassall, we have managed to stop up Jersey's vindictiveness. Now, it remains to confer with Sir Joseph as to how best we ought to proceed. I am inclined to believe that a father's affection for his lovely daughter will go far to assisting us in what remains to be done. Naturally, you are never to believe that I condone what you have done, but I understand the sense of injustice you experienced when I denied you a voucher. I, too, suffered when I realized how unfair the business was, especially as her ladyship of Jersey and I rarely see eye-to-eye on anything. In fact, I venture to say that I bear some blame in it. Had I seen to it that the voucher was promptly delivered to you, your entree into Almack's would have been unexceptional. Oh well, I do not see the profit in crying over spilt milk. The thing to do is to mop it up and right quickly. Now that your father is come, I dare say we shall see it through."

"My father, he is well? I cannot understand how he managed to come so quickly—"

"Again we have Henry to thank. They are, all of them, dropping with fatigue; your brother Christopher is with them as well, but my first concern was for Sir Joseph. I am relieved to be able to say that he stood up to the trip as well as any of them, so you need not worry yourself upon that score.

"Now, let us go down to the gentlemen. My lord is entertaining them until we come—and he is particularly interested to meet with you, your.g lady. He has always said that the trouble with the young people of today is that they have no enterprise—but do not let that bit of praise go to your head, young lady, for I say there has got to be a limit to enterprise before it takes on the nature of utter rashness."

"Yes, your ladyship," said Ann. If this was as bad a dusting as she was to suffer, she did not mind it at all.

When Ann followed Lady Cowper into the study, one glimpse of her father's distraught expression wrought such devastation in her breast that she broke away from her ladyship and threw herself down at her father's feet, crying: "Oh, Papa, I beg your forgiveness! I am filled with such shame and remorse, I c-cannot sp-speak!" and fell to weeping.

Christopher stared down at his sister, his forehead furrowed, his lips tight.

Henry, who had already risen, came quickly over

to her and brought her to her feet. "It is all right, my dear! There is no call for tears. As to regret, it wounds me deeply to learn that my efforts in your behalf gain me so little thanks. You have got your voucher, you have been to Almack's, and these, or so I understood it, were your dearest wishes."

"Lord Blayde," declared Sir Joseph. "You are an unregenerate scoundrel. I say you have taken foul advantage of my daughter, a weak female. How you can stand there without blenching, mouthing such insincere drivel, I cannot say, but this I do know, sir, you are unfit to share the same room, the same house with my daughter, despite that she has fallen so low!"

Henry, his face pale, turned to Ann. "And do you join with your father in these unpleasant sentiments?"

Ann's concern was for her father and his thought of her. She would not have dared to lower herself one step in his estimation, even if she had not thought that Henry's demeanor upon this occasion reeked of insolence. Her father was right. Henry showed not the least sign of repentance, and his words of consolation were without meaning. She had done wrong and now must suffer the consequences, consequences that were well understood by the world. As a rake, with rank, Henry would not reap the shameful crop that was to be hers. All the world understood that a female went off into the night with a gentleman to whom she was not wed, no, not even engaged, with the certain loss of whatever good name she possessed.

She went to stand by her father and, with her

hand upon his shoulder as he sat frowning at Henry, she said, coolly: "I do, sir."

Henry nodded, turned to Lady Cowper and said, calmly: "There is nothing more to be said. By your leave, my lady."

With that he bowed to all and withdrew.

Ann bit at her lip but to no avail. The tears would come and with them a wave of regret that this was the way it had to be. She would never see Henry again, and the thought made a tremendous wound in her heart.

Said Lady Cowper: "Ann, that was neither wise nor good of you. Sir Joseph, I know that you are distraught, but I pray you will consider what it is like to be young. I, sir, am not so far removed from your daughter's age that I do not recollect the impulsiveness of youth. In this instance, I would point out that there are all sorts of mitigating circumstances of which not the least is that Lord Blayde, for all his mien, is quite an honorable gentleman."

Sir Joseph made a gesture of protest and would have spoken, but Lady Cowper continued: "No, sir, I do not condone what these young people have been at, but it is more high-jinks than anything serious, and you must give credit to his lordship for making sure that, however it turned out, Ann would not suffer for it. I think that deserves a bit more thanks than he got from her."

"I am sure all you say is true, my lady, nor would I contradict you if it were not, because all that you have said has nothing to do with the case. Actually, it is my honor, the honor of the Keatings that has been stained by the thoughtless action of his lordship. I hold no brief for my daughter, she shares the same guilt. Now, we Keatings are made to look shameful and disgraced, all for what may be charitably described as a prank, a whim. No, your ladyship, I appreciate your point of view, but it is that of a female. We men have a stricter, uncompromising code of honor. Lord Blayde is guilty, but I am powerless to sit in judgment on him. Ann is guilty and, as she is my daughter, I *must* sit in judgment upon her. Who else is there?"

"Fiddlesticks, Sir Joseph! It is truly amazing how, while it is the man's duty to see to his honor, there is always some female who suffers for it. That, my dear sir, is neither honor nor gallantry! Here we have an innocent female—"

"Innocent, my lady?" asked Sir Joseph, "after such a night? Who would believe it?"

"Her father would, if he had an ounce of love, an ounce of respect, and an ounce of faith in his own flesh and blood."

Sir Joseph raised an eyebrow. "Christopher, here, is my son, and although we have as good an understanding as can be expected, still he is a wild youth. I have great love for him, and I have great faith that one day, he will be an unexceptional gentleman; but, for the moment until he arrives at that much-to-be-desired state, I would not trust him out of my eyesight—and with good reason! At the risk of my own embarrassment, I insist upon making it clear to you, Lady Cowper, that Christopher has been sent down from Oxford. So you see how troubled this parent is. Neither his son nor his daughter are anything to boast of."

"Ah!" exclaimed Lady Cowper with a delighted laugh. "I do agree. Children can be such a trial, it is a nine-days'-wonder that they ever manage to turn themselves into respected ladies and gentlemen. Truly, they owe so much to their parents."

The ghost of a smile tugged at the corner of Sir Joseph's mouth. "I understand quite well what you are saying, my lady; still, I am sure you will admit that misbehavior in the young cannot be condoned. In the case of my son, we have had a chat, and I am encouraged to believe that he will do better for himself at Oxford next year. But it is such a ticklish business with Ann."

Ann had been at his side, not having stirred since Henry had raised her to her feet. Now, Sir Joseph turned to her and said, kindly: "My dear, why do you not be seated. I have a feeling that this conversation will not be a short one."

Ann obeyed and he went on. "As I was saying, Lady Cowper, it is such a delicate business with a female. One has to step so carefully, and Ann is of an age to have understood how it is. I love my daughter, and my greatest wish is for her happiness. It drives me quite out of my mind to see how she has destroyed any prospect of granting me this wish for her."

Consolingly, Lady Cowper nodded and replied: "My dear Sir Joseph, having children of my own, I quite understand what is going through your mind. And, too, as I was much taken with your daughter—even to the extent of championing her cause before our Board and succeeding, mind you—my disappointment in Ann marches along with your own. Yet, I would not have her taste to the full the disgrace her misbehavior merits.

"There was a certain injustice in the treatment I meted out to her, and it takes no great insight into the matter to appreciate how it all went to encourage her in this regrettable episode. Now then, without condoning the young lady's actions, I would preserve her good name. That is the reason I did confer a voucher upon her after the fact and, at the same time, brought Lady Jersey round to approving it.

"It is all that is necessary to clear up the London end of the business, but I understand that the circumstances of Lord Blayde's and Ann's departure from your district left a great deal to be desired."

Sir Joseph had pursed his lips and was regarding her ladyship with an encouraging stare. "Hmmmm, I begin to see that you are more than a little disposed to be our friend in this matter, my lady."

"My dear Sir Joseph, more than friendship is at stake in this—and that is precisely what will save our Ann. But, for all that we have done here in the City, it will all be lost unless wagging tongues in Hertfordshire can be silenced as well."

Sir Joseph turned to Christopher. "I think it is just as well that Lord Blayde prevented you from going out to the Morgans' to inquire after your sister."

"He never prevented me, sir! I merely thought it was more important that he be attended to before anything else, the way in which he was skulking about—"

"Henry does not skulk, Christopher!" snapped Ann.

At once both Lady Emily and Sir Joseph turned their gaze upon her, and it was amusing to see that they both had raised their eyebrows in inquiry.

Ann was too embarrassed to see anything but the question in their eyes. She felt that she had to say something now in her own defense, especially as she was sure her face was as red as a rose.

"I mean to say," she said, "that Lord Blayde is just not the sort of person to do anything mean or underhanded—"

She had to stop at that point. Her audience had burst into laughter.

Then, as she realized how very untrue the latter part of her protest must sound, she could not forbear to chuckle herself.

Sir Joseph cleared his throat and remarked: "I dare say we can ignore that testimonial. Now then, if I may proceed, the question remains: How have the Morgans and their guests taken the fact of elopement? Perhaps they are not even aware of anything untoward having occurred."

"I think not, Papa. You see, it was quite the point of the party that Lord Blayde was to be there. As he was the guest of honor and Josephine Morgan was to be his partner, Henry's disappearance must have been remarked upon."

There was a very dissatisfied expression on Sir Joseph's face as he commented: "And it goes without saying that your absence, Mistress Keating, must have been as fully remarked. I do not think that Cheltenham will be quite far enough for us to escape the consequences of this dreadful eve. Ugh! I think a sojourn amongst the Irish is what is called for."

"Now, Sir Joseph, let us not be hasty!" chided her ladyship. "As I have said, more than Ann's reputation is at stake. We have come this far and it would appear that we have to proceed further with the business. Are you quite sure that you cannot stomach the presence of Lord Blayde at Tewin? I am sure it would make matters much easier."

Ann tried not to appear very interested, but her ears were keen to hear her father's reply.

"Indeed, my lady, I *am* quite sure of it. Still, I should like to hear what you have in mind."

"Actually, I am not pleased to suggest this, but circumstances are compelling. In effect, I propose to take precedence over the Morgans with Henry. He, I know, will make no objection, and the Morgans dare not. The way I see the matter is that Ann, Christopher, and yourself will return to Tewin in the Cowper coach; obviously, you had been sent for by me and had no choice but to come, regardless of your social commitments. Now then, if Henry were to join you in your return, it must be obvious that he, too, was made a part of your rush to London at my request. Truly, it will not be necessary that Lord Blayde stay for more than a day or two in the neighborhood. That will be sufficient time to put all the rumors to rest."

Sir Joseph thought over the Countess' proposal for a moment and then nodded his head.

"I venture to say that the arrangement is rather clever, my lady, and I will go so far as to permit Lord Blayde to return with us—"

Ann's gasp interrupted him so that he had to turn and look at her. With her face crimson once again, she subsided in confusion.

Said Sir Joseph: "If you have got something to say, child, I am sure we have the patience to attend you."

"Oh no, Papa. I was only thinking that Lady Cowper's scheme sounds perfectly sensible."

"I am not to happy to hear it called a 'scheme,' young lady," retorted her ladyship.

"I apologize to you, my lady."

The Countess sighed. "I do not suppose you truly ought to. At this moment, I dare say I am no better than you. Just see to what depths your conduct has brought all of us!"

"Indeed, my lady, I quite agree!" said Sir Joseph. "Now, as I was saying, it must be perfectly understood by Lord Blayde that while we may give the appearance of being social, he is on his honor to take no advantage of the fact. He will give the appearance of calling upon us and we shall, all of us, act the parts that are called for—but that is all. As far as the Keatings are concerned, he is not welcomed, he is merely tolerated for appearance's sake. If he can be made to understand that, then I am in accord with you, my lady."

"Excellent! By your leave, Sir Joseph, I am going to request that Christopher be my emissary to his lordship. I believe haste is all important in this. There is no time for an exchange of notes. Someone has to go out to his lordship and return with him, so that all may be put in order without delay."

"You would send Christopher?" asked Sir Joseph, regarding his son with grave doubt.

"Oh, not Christopher!" exclaimed Ann, scornfully.

"Why not Christopher?" demanded young Mr. Keating, rising and glaring at his sister.

"Yes, why not Christopher?" agreed Lady Cowper. "It is beneath your dignity, Sir Joseph, especially in the light of your last remark to his lordship. It is beyond anything to even think of Ann going to him, and I dare not ask my lord to become involved in it—"

"Thank you, my dear," put in the Earl of Cowper for the first time. "Much as I am entertained by this great tribulation, I am happy to continue in my capacity of dumb observer."

Lady Cowper smiled at him and then turned to Sir Joseph. "So you see, it is not something I care to entrust to a servant, leaving Christopher as our favorite messenger."

"Oh, I say!" exclaimed Christopher. "What I mean to say is I am not sure I care for the honor. Lord Blayde and I are not upon the best of terms, to put it mildly."

Lady Cowper looked at him in surprise. "Well, really, Christopher, but a moment ago you were insisting that it was quite the thing!"

"Your ladyship, I had only intended to point out that there was nothing exceptional in my being a candidate for the embassy. I did not mean to insist that I be elected—"

"Oh, but you were, dear boy! I elected you, we all elected you! Did we not, Sir Joseph?"

The Baronet raised a weary hand to brush at the gray locks overhanging his brow. He looked at Lord Cowper who merely winked at him.

Turning back to his son, he shrugged and said: "My boy, the Countess has a deal more faith in your diplomatic talents than do I. I pray that I may learn a lesson of her, rather than she of me."

Christopher groaned and reluctantly got to his feet.

Although Ann's expression did not show a hint of approval, within, her heart was singing.

CHAPTER 14

Christopher was directed to Holland House where, Lady Cowper had informed him, Lord Blayde maintained a residence with his aunt, Lady Holland. It was out on the Kensington Road and Christopher was not at his brightest, feeling very strongly that it was not a mission he would have welcomed even after a night of peaceful rest.

Holland House was not easy to miss. The estate upon which it sat was quite extensive and served as a fit setting for the palatial residence. As he was driven up the drive in the Cowper carriage, he felt overwhelmed by the great building with its triple towers and its Jacobean gables, decorated with lacy parapets of stone that quite failed to disguise a certain massive stolidness. Yet, as compared to anything he had been close to in Hertfordshire and in Oxford, it was a most impressive pile.

The great circular drive which extended almost to the full breadth of the vast front could easily have served as a racetrack for two carriages or four horses, thought Christopher, and he felt so overborne by the high-gabled structure, he prayed that no one would be within to receive him.

The carriage came smartly to a stop before the front portico in the center of which, and attached to the building behind, reared a tower whose base housed the main front entrance. It must have been added as an afterthought, for its styling was baroque in contrast to the uninspiring Jacobean textures at its back.

Much to Christopher's annoyance but not to his expectation, the Cowper footman returned with the information that Lady Holland would receive him.

Taking this to be some slight misunderstanding, Christopher dismounted from the carriage and entered the house, girding his mental loins for the encounter with Lord Blayde.

He was led into a room of vast dimension that might have served as a dining room, but that was appointed as a lady's sitting room on a lavish scale. Once again he felt dwarfed by his surroundings, only this time it was even worse, for there was a veritable queen of a grande dame awaiting him with a haughty air. She was seated upon a chaise longue, semireclining on her side, her feet over the edge and resting on a fine decorative stool. At her elbow was a neat little table, a match to the stool, holding a small collection of sweetmeats and notepapers.

His heart sank. He had no stomach to meet the famous Lady Holland. For one thing he had not the polish nor the experience to deal with a lady whom everyone accounted the de facto leader of London Society.

He made the best bow that he could and said: "I beg your pardon, Lady Holland, but my business is not with your ladyship."

Her bright eyes opened wide and a smile lit up her handsome face.

"How very ungallant of you to say so, Mr. Keating. Even if he did not mean it, a gentleman would never say as much. Do you find me so repulsive that you cannot spare me a few minutes of your time?"

Christopher smiled sheepishly and stammered: "N-not at all, my lady! I never meant that I should be displeased at the prospect. It is just that I thought it had been misunderstood that I came a-purpose to have a conversation with Lord Blayde and was, therefore, intruding upon you."

Lady Holland cocked her head and looked doubtful. "Well, it was not so nicely done, but I shall let you off this time. After all, one must consider the source before one can judge the depth of the compliment, mustn't one."

"I pray that you will do so, my lady."

"Very well. Now do not stand about as though your limbs could not support you, and find yourself a seat. Lord Blayde has been summoned, but I cannot vouch for the fact that he will receive you. He has had a most difficult night, as I understand it, and is still hard asleep. In fact, it was not so long ago that he came in."

At the word sleep, Christopher could not suppress a yawn. Before he could apologize, her ladyship was on him.

"I must say, Mr. Keating, you are quite the most uncomplimentary gentleman it has been my duty to entertain. I am sure that no one has ever showed such signs of ennui in my presence before!"

Her eyes were snapping and she was angry.

"I beg your pardon, my lady, but nature will not be denied. I have had as little rest as his lordship this night and the very idea of retiring is quite overwhelming—"

She frowned. "Then it must be rather important business you have got with Lord Blayde. I thought you were but a friend."

"I can assure you that we are *not* friends!" said Christopher, rather emphatically.

"Heavens! Then you must be enemies! Mr. Keating, if you are serving as someone's second, I must ask you to leave at once! I do not tolerate dueling or other such nonsense—"

"No, no, your ladyship, it is nothing like that at all. I come bearing a message for his lordship from the Countess of Cowper—"

"From Emily?" exclaimed Lady Holland. "How delightful! Why did you not say so at once, dear boy? What does the dear Countess have to say?"

Christopher swallowed hard and blushed. Before he could respond, Lady Holland's delighted laughter rang through the chamber.

"It is for an assignation, isn't it? Oh, you need not say a word more to me. I always thought that Emily nursed a *tendre* for my nephew. Quickly now, Mr. Keating, what is the message? I am dying to hear it!"

It was not so much a battle of wits as it was

what threatened to become an utter rout. Fatigue was dulling Christopher's brain, and the lady was most fetching. The thought of an assignation with Lady Holland ran through his mind, giving rise to a strong impulse to grant her every wish. It was with the greatest effort that Christopher explained: "I would not disappoint you for the world, my lady, but I do assure you that you misjudge the situation. I am here in the interest of my sister, you see—"

Lady Holland's face fell. "Then it is not Emily but a Miss Keating, Henry has got himself entangled with. How utterly boring! But you say that you are not come seeking vengeance, Mr. Keating? Pray how am I to understand Lady Cowper's part in all of this—or do you have a penchant for using other people's good names for your own purposes?"

"No, no, Lady Holland, it is nothing like that at all!" exclaimed Christopher in tones of pain. "Really, it is not—but I cannot explain the matter to you, for it is a most private business."

"What could be more private than an illicit union, young man?" she demanded.

Christopher reached into his pocket and tore forth from it a handkerchief which he immediately applied to his brow. His weary mind raced for the words to put off Lady Holland's curiosity without offending her and, above all, without encouraging her in her scandalous opinion.

"Keating! What the devil are you dong here?" demanded a voice from behind. Lord Blayde, his hair tousled and his face unshaven, came into the room in his dressing gown. There was a dark scowl on his face as he demanded: "Why in Lucifer's name are you not abed? Surely there are chambers aplenty at the Cowper residence!"

"Henry, what is all this about? I demand to know," cried Lady Holland, sitting up. "Who is this Miss Keating and why have I never heard of her?"

Wearily, Henry looked at Christopher as he addressed her ladyship: "What has this whelp been telling you, Bess?"

Christopher, who had been seated, very ill at ease, leaped to his feet.

"Lord Blayde, you have no right to insult the brother of the lady you have compromised! If you persist, I shall have no recourse but to demand satisfaction!"

"Oh, go to the devil! Bess, I assure you whatever he has told you, it is all of it exaggeration. I assure you it is a most simple business to explain— But I am damned if I shall go to the bother. A tempest in a teapot, nothing more!"

With that, he plumped himself down into the nearest chair, leaving Christopher bristling with anger, his mouth trying to frame a retort that would slay the Viscount.

"I do declare this is most interesting, Henry," said Lady Holland. "The morning is turning into something far more interesting than I should have guessed. Now, you must give me all of the details, especially how it comes that Lady Cowper has managed to inveigle herself into the midst of it all."

Henry turned to Christopher and exclaimed: "What, must you unburden your liver to the first one you meet, and she the greatest gossip of them all?"

"Another such fine compliment, Lord Blayde, and I shall positively blush!" snapped her ladyship, her eyes sparkling angrily.

Henry groaned. "My lady, I beg you will excuse the two of us. I do not think that what this pup has to say does concern you. If it should, you may rest assured that I will inform you—"

"Not on your life shall I excuse you, Henry! I want to know every detail of this wretched business—"

"It is not wretched no matter what Keating has told you, madam! It is simply a case of doing a favor for a person and receiving gross ingratitude in return—"

"A favor? That is a whopper, Blayde!" retorted Christopher.

"Look you, Keating, she desired a voucher to Almack's and I got it for her, did I not?"

"How do you come to give out vouchers for Almack's, Henry?" demanded Lady Holland. "Even I have not that privilege—not but what I could have it if I wished."

"Bess, it is a long story, and I am sure you would find its narration quite boring—"

"I am sure I should not!" she retorted. "If it has any bearing upon our good name, I demand to know."

"Lord Blayde, I forbid it!" declared Christopher. "It is my sister's good name that is at stake!"

"It appears to me that you have already drooled all over your bib, my lad. I do not see that her ladyship's wish can compromise Ann anymore than you already have."

"So! Her name is Ann, Ann Keating," commented Lady Holland, with interest.

Henry grinned. "She is a sharp one. See how much she knows? You must have told her far more than was needed."

Christopher looked troubled. "I assure you I did not, my lord. But you are making it all more than plain to her with your thoughtless remarks. I beg you to assure her ladyship that whatever has taken place, it was of the most innocent nature. She does not appear to believe me."

"Oh, I say, Bess, is this true? Do you think it is anything more than a most innocent caper?"

"What am I to think? You are, the both of you, most secretive about the details of whatever it is that has occurred, and the more you say, the more I am led to believe that you, my lord, have seduced a female who is, for all I know of her, no better than she should be."

Henry let out a groan. "Ye gods, man, what did you say to Lady Holland? My brain is reeling with exhaustion. I am not in any fit condition to take the stand in defense of Ann's and my reputations."

"I think, my lord, you better had," said Lady Holland. "I was hoping for some juicy morsel, but I am willing to settle for just a clarification of what is going on."

"Very well, but after I have done explaining, I am off to bed and to sleep for a week!"

"I beg your pardon, Lord Blayde, but that will not be possible. Lady Cowper has sent me with express purpose of fetching you back," said Christopher.

"Devil take Lady Cowper!"

"Now, now, Henry, that is not a very nice thing to say about so charming a lady," admonished Lady Holland. "Come, there's a good fellow! Tell your auntie all about it, and then we shall consult together as to what needs be done."

"Oh, do not try to butter me up, Bess! I shall make what explanation I deem is necessary for your fair ears, but that is all! I am dead with fatigue, and Lady Cowper can do what she pleases so long as it is without me!"

With that, he went off into a narration of the last evening's events, every now and then having to pause to consult with Christopher for some detail.

Lady Holland listened with the greatest patience to all he had to say and, by the time he had ended his tale, she was all smiles.

"My, oh my, how very delicious it all is!" she exclaimed. "Truly, Henry you have done it all to a turn. I venture to say that Miss Keating's reputation will not be worth a farthing, and you shall have all the pleasure of being known as a blackguard with none of the profit. How very sweet!"

"Only, my lady, if you cannot keep a guard upon your tongue," he shot back.

"But I am sure that Sarah will have bruited it about before the sun sets this day, so why must I be denied the pleasure of carrying the news?"

"Because Lady Jersey has no interest in the story making the rounds. It would spell disaster for her pet establishment. You know how fiercely she guards Almack's."

"But, my dear nephew, that is precisely why I would take advantage of the situation. Sarah is so high in the instep about everything, it would give me the greatest pleasure to see her taken down a peg."

"Along with your nephew and innocent Miss Keating?"

"I have only your word for Miss Keating's innocence, Henry."

By this time Christopher was almost in tears. "Oh, I say, your ladyship, you cannot destroy it all!"

"Now, look you, Bess, I can assure you the story will never make the rounds unless you wish it. None of us, including Sarah, has the least desire to have it noised about. Consider that Lady Cowper had already made up her mind to grant a voucher to Ann, and Lady Sarah was forced to approve. Whatever malicious pleasure it will give you to declare it all to the world cannot compensate for the damage that will be done to Almack's, the Keatings and, not the least, to the Vassalls, of which last you are a member, Auntie."

"Henry, you are quite the spoilsport. Ah me, it will be a terrible temptation to put behind me, but I dare say, if Sarah can resist it, so can I. But it appears to me that while everyone's mouth may be stopped here in London, what will be said in Tewin and Ware and Hertford?"

At this juncture, Christopher put in: "My lady, that is precisely why I am come. I must needs fetch Lord Blayde back with me so that he can return to Hertfordshire with Ann, my father, and myself, to make all appearances unexceptional. Lady Cowper has graciously condescended to make it appear that she summoned us all to London on no notice at all."

"Poor Mrs. Morgan," remarked Lady Holland. "How put upon must she feel when she learns that her guest of honor was peremptorily commanded away from her party."

"I do not think that that is at all necessary!" intervened Henry. *"Emily's* presence is all that is needed, and I am tired to death of the entire business. I want my rest!"

"Oh, you poor little boy!" said Lady Holland, pityingly. "Shall ittums be cwoss if ittums does not have Nanny to tuck ittums in? Henry, behave yourself! If Emily is willing to take such pains for you and Miss Keating, you have no choice. I, for one, am puzzled to know what is behind her fine Italian hand. Which of you is of more concern to her, Miss Keating or you—or is it the both of you together that has her interest?"

"Lord Blayde, can you not see the necessity for you joining us in our return to Hertfordshire?" asked Christopher earnestly.

"All I can see is the necessity for gaining my rest! Have you any idea how many times I have had to traverse the road to Hertfordshire within the last twelve hours?"

Lady Holland studied her nephew for a moment.

"Do you know how you sound, Henry?" she asked, her eyebrows raised slightly.

"Indeed!" he snorted. "You are about to inform me that I sound like a child, petulant from lack of sleep! Look you, madam, I only did as requested for the Keatings and was repaid with neither a smile nor with thanks. I feel that I am not obliged any further in the matter."

"No, Lord Blayde," responded Lady Holland, "not a child, rather a gentleman who has been crossed. You like the lady, do you not?"

Christopher showed his incredulity with a smirk.

"I would have hardly gone to so much trouble had I despised her," Henry growled. "But I do not see what that has to do with anything. My services to the lady were received with anger and disdain. One would have thought that I risked naught in the business. Ah, what can one expect? Some people are never satisfied."

"So this is what my brilliant and charming nephew has come to, is it? You have put a lady's good fame in jeopardy, and now you resent the fact that she is upset and regards you with fear and trembling."

Henry could not repress a chuckle. "Ann does not strike me as being timorous. Quite the contrary. I venture to say that there are not many females of her breeding with the nerve to have accepted my offer. Actually, I am pleased that I *did* succeed with the *voucher* business—and that was more than I had promised. I only undertook to give her an evening at Almack's. Now she has got two Countesses in her pocket. I have the greatest faith that Jersey and Cowper will see to it that Ann's name remains untarnished. There is no need for me to continue in the business—especially as Ann has made her opinion of me very clear."

"Hmmm. You talk a good game, Nephew; but it seems to me that you have been given a setdown by a snip of a girl and fear another at her hands. I suggest that you examine your own feelings in the matter and begin to act like a man and not a schoolboy. It is more than time that you did, Viscount Blayde."

"Bess, you are making too much of the business. What are you at? I do not see that it is any concern of yours whether I go back to my slumbers at this point, or travel out to Hertfordshire with the Keatings."

"Then I shall explain carefully my feelings in the matter. Here am I having to hold my tongue over the juiciest bit of gossip to come my way in many a moon, and you are about to ruin everything. How shall I look when the word comes back to London from Ware of your elopement? I shall look a fool because I shall appear to know nothing of it and my own nephew involved. Henry, I demand that you do as Emily wishes in this matter. She, as well as Sarah, has an interest to protect in this, and I am willing to rely upon her judgment as to what is necessary. You, my nephew, are about to travel back to Hertfordshire, sleep or no—since the female in the case is of no further interest to you, you can act the boor and sleep all the way—but go you shall!"

Her answer was a growl and a glare. Then Henry looked at Christopher and said: "My lad, we are *not* well met. If you can be patient for an hour, I shall attempt to make myself look decent and we shall go off together to Lady Cowper's."

He stood up, scowled at his aunt, and nodded, as Christopher arose, too, saying: "Thank you, my lord. We Keatings shall be forever in your debt."

He snorted and, as he departed, flung over his shoulder: "I do not see why. But for me, the mess we are in would never have occurred."

There was a wise smile on Lady Holland's face as she watched her nephew stride out of the room, tearing at the scarf about his neck. She turned to Christopher and said: "Mr. Keating, I regret that

I have never had the pleasure of meeting your sister. Perhaps you will be kind enough to tell me something about her. It will do to while away the time whilst we await His Majesty to complete his toilet."

CHAPTER 15

The traveling coach of the Cowpers was a splendid vehicle. Every comfort that a traveler might desire was ready at hand or designed to surround and support the occupants unbidden. Hand-tooled squabs upholstered by artisans who knew how to work the supplest leather to its fittest use put the passengers at ease. Nor were the great leather springs far behind in their ability to control the sway of the cab or dampen the roughness of the road. Even the lights were made of plate glass to give an undistorted view of the country they were passing through. And if, as was the case with Ann, a breath of fresh air was needed, the panes slid down surely but gently so that even the weakest female would have no trouble in manipulating them.

The carriage was designed to hold six passengers in the greatest comfort, but it was only partially filled. Sir Joseph was reclining on the forward seat all by himself. The night of agitation and the uncertain morning that had followed it had taken their toll of the poor man. His face was drawn with fatigue and the strain showed even as he slept in the sight of the three passengers seated opposite.

Had he been able to keep his weary eyes open, he might have been shocked into a more awake posture, for the sight of Ann at the window with Lord Blayde's dark head resting on her shoulder was more than enough to have given him pause.

His lordship was as soundly asleep as was Sir Joseph, and Christopher, too, who was in the window seat to his right.

Of them all, only Ann was awake and that was understandable, since she was the only one who had had a night's rest. What was not so understandable was the atmosphere that pervaded the cab of the vehicle.

With all that slumber being enjoyed, there should have been a very restful air that might have encouraged Ann to doze off, too. But that was not the case.

Ann was sensible of the strain, not only of the weight upon her shoulder but of the aloofness of the head whose weight she was bearing toward her, an aloofness heavily tinted with animosity.

Further, she knew that Sir Joseph had not said his last word to her about the previous night's episode, and she was not looking forward to the time when he would summon her into his study for a grave and lengthy lecture.

Ann was upset as was to be expected. Things

between her father and herself could never be the same again. It was a matter of trust and she had failed Sir Joseph in it.

As for Henry, it was as true with him. Things could never be the same between them. He had, by the skin of his teeth, managed to salvage her name in this business; but, in doing so, he had brought to her all manner of troubles. He ought to have been repentant and begged her forgiveness. Instead, he had assumed an arrogance that was downright insolent, so that her annoyance with him was beyond what was called for under the circumstances.

It only made her more angry to see him come into the Cowpers' residence like some great savior, making odious sacrifice in the Keatings' behalf.

One would have thought it had been her idea to have him accompany them home. It was all of Lady Cowper's doing, and it was to her that this noble oaf should have made his complaint. But no, he had pulled a long face with her, had responded to her cheery greeting with a faint sneer, and had very little to say thereafter to her.

Of course, he had had very little to say to anyone, for he had deposited himself into a chair and fallen right asleep until it was time to leave.

Yes, he was very tired and, of course, he had every right to be. Why the poor man had driven this very route three times himself, and now was embarked upon it for a fourth time in less than a day's span!

Ann swallowed hard. For some reason, she found the thought particularly troubling. As much as she was upset with Henry, her conscience insisted upon meting out to herself a fuller share of the blame. She had had no right to have encouraged Henry in the adventure. She was no silly schoolgirl to have been so easily swept off her feet into a circumstance that could not help but redound to her discredit! Actually, Henry had every right to be annoyed with her—but *not* for *his* reasons!

Why must he believe that she owed him anything at all? He had fallen just as deeply as she had into the mire of ill-fame, and it was as much to his advantage to escape the consequences as to hers. They both of them ought to have shared the blame or the credit—although there was no credit in it.

But Henry was as unreasonable as he was wild, and there was no talking to him. Now he was engaged in what he had termed "an onerous duty," as if it would not help to clear his name as well. Ann was filled with resentment and, if Henry's head had been but an ounce heavier on her shoulder, she was sure she would have shrugged it off with a vigor to have awakened him sharply.

She looked over at her father. His handsome face was more relaxed now that sleep had helped restore him. Still, there was a wanness in the cheeks and a strain about the closed eyes that tugged at her heart, making her own eyes go moist. What a horrid daughter he had!

Despite appearances, Henry was not deep in slumber, yet he was far from awake. Rather, he was in a state somewhere between, fitfully dozing, pervaded by such languor that he felt not the least inclination to change his position. He knew very well that his head was resting upon Ann's soft shoulder and the fact did not disturb him. He was very much aware of her proximity and it rather pleased him to take advantage of his weariness to thus impose upon her. He fancied that the debt she owed him was being repaid, even if unconsciously so on her part.

Not that he had any intention of exacting a greater tribute from her. The less he had to do with her, once this ridiculous journey was over and the business done with, the better. Although he might have withstood Lady Cowper's demands that he accompany the Keatings, Lady Holland, his aunt and the factual head of the Vassalls, was not a lady one willfully crossed.

He was still quite proud of himself for having succeeded so well, and gloated over all the invitations to dine he would receive once rumors started to fly.

No, he did not intend to start them himself, for he was honor bound to secrecy; but he knew Jersey and Cowper and Bess very well. None of them could hold a secret, he was sure.

He shifted his position slightly as a thought made him uneasy. It had to do with Ann. When the story finally did come out, she was bound to suffer for it. There was no way to explain or excuse the fact that she had been alone with him, unchaperoned, for so many hours at night. Suddenly he was anxious to see how she was standing up to it. He opened one eye.

Their faces were very close, closer than they had ever been. On Ann's lips, a bemused smile lingered as she gazed down at Henry, his head at rest upon her shoulder. She saw his eyelid lift partway and she knew he was awake. She knew she should start back in great embarrassment but her impulse was to stay as she was. Henry did not stir either, his eye now open, his other still buried against her, his attention fastened on her full lips.

For a moment, it was as though no one else shared the coach with them and their faces moved closer.

Then Henry, recovering himself, jerked himself upright, murmuring an apology while Ann moved away from him, her cheeks growing pink.

Henry frowned and Ann turned her head to peer out of the window.

"I say, where have we got to?" asked Henry in a tone he tried to make conversational.

"I have not the vaguest notion, my lord."

Henry bent his head to look out, too. "Ah yes, we have come a fair piece. Cheshunt, I am sure. A little beyond, I make it."

"Hush, you will awaken the others!" hissed Ann. At which, both Sir Joseph and Christopher stirred themselves awake.

The latter stretched and yawned. "Are we there?"

Sir Joseph smiled across the cab and began to straighten his clothing.

"I pray you rested well, Papa," said Ann.

"Yes, I did. It is a marvelously well-constructed machine. Comfortable as a cradle. And you, my lord?"

"Thank you, sir, I have recovered somewhat. I believe we have about ten miles remaining."

Christopher looked out of the window. "We are well past Cheshunt, Dad."

Sir Joseph made a face. "The things you have learned at the University do no credit to the institution. Dad? Pfagh! If you cannot say Father, then address me as Sir Joseph. I should feel a deal more comfortable, despite you are my son."

"Regrets and all that sort of thing, Father," said Christopher with a grin. "I say, do you know I think I was never happier to see the place than I shall be when we arrive. About an hour's time I think."

"It will be longer than that, my boy. We have first to stop at the Morgans and then let his lordship out at Panshanger—"

"Damnation! I clean forgot that little business!" exclaimed Henry. "What the devil am I to say to them?"

Christopher piped up: "Now you know how I felt having to call upon *you,* my lord, at Holland House. These things are neither easy nor pleasant."

Henry ignored him and looked to Ann. "I have a slight suspicion that Emily cooked up some sort of explanation for me to deliver to those worthy people but, for the life of me, I cannot recall a word of it."

"Lady Cowper had matters of great importance to impart to my family and sent you as emissary to fetch us," replied Ann.

"I have been thinking," said Sir Joseph, "and it does not appear to me that it will wash. I mean to say, there was Lord Blayde in the neighborhood. How did he come to receive such a command from the Countess?"

"Obviously, I received an express, sir."

"What, at the party? I am reasonably certain no one observed the nonexistent messenger," Sir Joseph pointed out.

"It was I, sir," said Christopher. "I carried the message, and snatched Lord Blayde and Ann away. That will wash, I am sure."

Sir Joseph nodded his approval. "There you have it, my lord. It is all quite simple."

Henry made a face. "I do not like to prevaricate."

Ann chuckled. "Oh, what a whopper that is!" she burst forth.

Henry looked angrily at her. "That is most unkind of you, Miss Keating!"

"I was only thinking that our visit to Almack's was based upon lies from beginning to end, and you appeared to enjoy it all immensely, *your lordship*."

"I can assure you it is not the same thing! I should say it was all pretense rather than out-and-out lying. I never *said* that you were my sister."

"You did not have to. If I held Lady Horatia's voucher and you, your lordship, were at ease at my side, whom else could I be taken for?"

"I tell you it is not the same, Miss Keating."

"I tell you it is!"

"Now, now, let us not have any unpleasantness," Sir Joseph intervened. "Heaven knows we have still a few steps left to complete in this business, which at best is something a deal less than pleasant already."

"You cannot imagine how happy I shall be when it is over and done with," said Henry, glowering at Ann.

"Indeed, your lordship, I could not agree more!" retorted Ann.

Which left nothing more to be said. Sir Joseph

shrugged, Christopher made a face, and Henry, with a sulky look upon his countenance, gave himself over to his coming meeting with the Morgans.

Ann was disgusted. One would have thought that by this time, Henry would have recovered himself sufficiently to put a good face upon it. But no, he was quite content to pretend he was still not much to blame, and behave himself in a high-nosed fashion. What an odious outcome it all would have been for her had not Lady Cowper practically forced him to return with them. Actually she was inclined to wonder that he should have acceded to her request at all. It was legend that one could never hope an irresponsible rake would go to the pains of making amends for his mischief no matter who might demand it of him.

She gave a quick little glance to the side to see what he was about and decided that, still, even all dark and brooding as he was at that moment, he was a most attractive fellow, and there had to be some good in him. She recalled him as he was as they had entered the famous Assembly Room. It was at that point she had wished that it had been all genuine, she not his make-believe sister but the lady he had chosen, proud for all the world to meet her.

It was beyond all possibility that that wish could ever be granted, and it did not stay with her for very long. They had been parted almost immediately and Lady Jersey's summons had brought the curtain down upon the entire masquerade. Whatever pleasure she might have had was thoroughly ruined, and so badly that even the lagniappe of a proper voucher, which ought to have thrilled her beyond measure, was transformed into a pointless gift. She never expected to make use of it.

They arrived in Ware and soon were traveling up the drive to Brickden Bury to make the momentous call upon the Morgans.

CHAPTER 16

Two days passed and it took all that much time for Sir Joseph to recuperate from the anguish and the physical strain he had had to endure. Fortunately, whatever Mrs. Morgan may have thought of events, the Cowper coach and Lord Blayde's explanation and apology satisfied her that the Countess of Cowper had ruined her party quite unintentionally when she had so summarily drawn Lord Blayde away from the festivities she was sponsoring. Since his lordship was empowered to extend an invitation from Lady Cowper to the Morgans to call upon her when next they were in London, Mrs. Morgan's disappointment was quite overcome by the prospect of visiting a higher circle than to which she had been hitherto privileged.

It eased the hearts of the Keatings to see how well Ann's misbehavior could be made to appear in an unexceptional light. But neither Ann nor her father was bound to forget that it had ever occurred.

During the two days that Sir Joseph spent in his bed, gradually restoring his energies, Ann was left to ponder upon what his first words might be to her on the subject. Considering the ordeal she had already put him through she was not prepared for any sort of a vehement discussion. Whatever Sir Joseph had in mind for her, she would accept without a murmur. For one thing, it could not be more than she deserved, nor dared she allow herself the least defense for her actions. It would serve no purpose but to exhaust her father.

A blue mood had settled upon her, and that, try as she might, she could not shake off. She tried to assure herself that it was due solely to how unhappy she had made her father, but she could not hide the fact that, as she watched Henry drive away to Panshanger in the Cowper coach, her heart had dipped low in her breast.

He was an impossible man, he was an insolent man, he was arrogance personified; but she knew that he could be merry and he could be kind. She recalled his manner when he had first approached her on the business of the voucher. How warmed she had felt, believing his interest had been in her. Oh, if only it had been, they would never have had to fall out with each other!

Yes, that was it! It was his attitude throughout the entire episode that had brought her feelings to an antagonistic pitch. Not once during their ride to London, not once after they had arrived at Almack's, had there been any sign of a tender feeling between them, no, not even a tender word.

All she had been to him was the means by which he could tease the Ladies of Almack's, and devil take herself for all he cared!

She reached into her pocket and drew out the small bit of paper that Lady Cowper had given to her. It was rather crinkled and she placed it on her knee, carefully smoothing it out.

Such a fateful bit of foolscap! For any but herself, it was the key to the rarefied precincts of a superior world. For herself, it was but a reminder, a recrimination, of the disgrace she had earned; yet the bitter fruits of which she had escaped tasting to the full. All of her life, it would be the sorriest of souvenirs to bring back to her mind's eye that which she hoped everyone would forget.

But it was more than that. There was another sort of pain connected with the voucher: the memory of Henry Vassall. Now that he was quite gone out of her life, she could afford to admit to herself that, had he been a slightly different sort, she could have fallen madly in love with him. As it was, she could never be sure that she had not, if only for an instant.

But it was not a question to be proposed nor to be answered. Henry had not called. It was two days since he had left the Keatings upon the threshold of their home. Not that she had expected that he would. Undoubtedly, he had set himself down at Panshanger for a day's rest after all the driving and riding he had had to do, and then taken the Cowper coach back to London. Considering how distant and cool were the attitudes of Sir Joseph and Christopher toward him, and considering how Henry matched their manners, the constrained leave-taking at their door must signal the last connection between Viscount Blayde and the Keating family.

Then, too, Ann was reminded that now the move to Cheltenham must proceed apace. This must put the quietus to even the slight prospect of their meeting by chance. Cheltenham was so far from London that she doubted if Henry had ever visited the place. She had the distinct impression that Panshanger was as far as he had ever managed to remove himself from the metropolis.

She sighed and went up to bid her father goodnight before retiring.

At breakfast, the following morning, Ann was pleased to sit down with her father and Christopher, for Sir Joseph was looking well and was able to dismiss his children's concern by saying he had only lost a great deal of sleep which had to be made up. Then he entered into a discussion with Christopher as to what the young man's plans were for the ensuing months before he would be allowed back into the University.

Apparently Christopher had been aware of his father's concern and was able to reassure Sir Joseph that he would not rest idly by. He had brought his books with him and would continue with his studies so that the time would not be wasted. Much to his dismay, his father carried the business one step further. He knew of an instructor connected with the Blue Coat School in Hertford who would be only too pleased to take Christopher under his wing and direct his studies. Upon receiving the news of his son's having been sent down, Sir Joseph had entered into a correspondence with the schoolmaster and had been directed to this gentleman. Christopher would have to walk the three and a half miles into town three days a week because Sir Joseph could not spare the carriage.

"Into town?" asked Christopher. "Why cannot he come out to us here?"

"For the good and simple reason that Mr. Pedley's duties at the school will not permit it. Furthermore, whatever in the nature of books and foolscap is needed will be readily available at the school to assist you in executing the exercises Mr. Pedley sees fit to assign to you."

"But, Father, that is a child's school! I am from the University. Do you expect me to sit amongst a gang of riotous schoolboys, years younger than myself—"

"Don't be an ass! Obviously, you and Mr. Pedley will repair to his rooms where he can tutor you in private. I pray you will not make any objection for my mind is quite set upon it."

"But what of Cheltenham? How am I to proceed if you remove us to Cheltenham?"

"At this pass, Cheltenham is quite out of the question for the Keatings. Your sister Ann has seen to that."

"But, Papa, I should be only too happy to remove to Cheltenham, if that is your desire," said Ann, bracing herself for the lecture that must follow.

Sir Joseph sighed and shook his head. "No, we cannot move from this place yet. It would only cause many questions to be asked. We should look as though we were fleeing from something. Then, despite Lady Cowper's assurances and Lord Blayde's apologies that have already been made, all that was said and done will begin to appear in an odd light. Actually, none of it will stand up under a close scrutiny, and our remaining on the spot, as it were, will put off such scrutiny as curiosity might suggest in our absence. One cannot be too cautious when a reputation is involved. It is quite a delicate thing, you know—and that is something I never thought I should have to point out to the daughter of my heart."

Ann hung her head and said, meekly: "Yes, Papa."

Sir Joseph went on. "I have not done with you, young lady."

He cleared his throat, rested his arms upon the table, leaned forward, and began: "At the outset, my child, you must know that I love you dearly and—"

One of the maid-servants came into the dining room and laid a folded and sealed note down before Sir Joseph. Then she stood back, hugging herself while she waited.

"What is this?" asked Sir Joseph. "Is an answer required?"

"Yes, sir. The footman from they Cowpers be waitin'."

Sir Joseph excused himself, opened up the note, and frowned as he perused it.

"How very odd!" he murmured.

"Is it from Lady Cowper? She has returned?" inquired Ann.

"No, my dear, she has not returned and it is from Lord Blayde, who I was sure had departed the district days ago."

"Henry Vassall? He is still about?"

"Quite, and he is asking that I receive him in the morning."

Ann's pulse quickened. "Shall you receive him, Papa?"

"I am reluctant to do so, but I do not see that I have any choice in the matter."

Ann swallowed hard. "I had thought that he had had quite enough of us. What is it to be, Papa, a social visit?"

Sir Joseph shook his head. "No, it is more in the nature of a business visit, and it concerns, oddly enough—"

"Yes, Papa?" gasped Ann.

"Christopher, here."

"Me? He wants to speak with me? Whatever for?" exclaimed Christopher.

"He expresses a wish to speak to the both of us I assume. The business has to do with your future endeavors, young man."

Christopher sat back and sneered: "What has my future to do with Lord Blayde, I should like to know."

"Well, that is precisely what we shall find out when the gentleman comes calling tomorrow morning, shan't we."

He turned to the maid. "Inform the Cowpers' man that I should be pleased to grant Lord Blayde's request."

She left and Ann asked: "Is that all he had to say on the note?"

Her father replied: "He ended it with his regards, my dear."

"To whom, may I ask?"

"To all of us, of course."

"Oh," said Ann.

Never had Ann experienced so sad a disappointment. He could have, at the very least, mentioned her by name. But he had not included her in the note at all. As far as he was concerned she no longer had any existence in his eyes. But what in heaven's name was his completely unlooked-for interest in Christopher? Why, she had never heard them exchange a word but it was in a most chilly and forbidding manner.

Perhaps Henry was out to seek revenge upon the Keatings for having put him through so arduous an ordeal. After all, she did not know him so very well, and had hardly seen him at his best. Henry Vassall might actually be quite a villain!

The thought could not survive her true feelings. Henry was not that sort of fellow. He could be cold and distant, that she knew from experience. He could be angry, even unjustifiably so, but he was not mean and vicious. That she could never truly believe of him.

Still, he was coming to Tewin on the morrow and she must see him, even if he had made it unmistakably clear that he wished no dealings with herself. Well, she had no wish to deal with him either, and she would show her feelings on the matter every bit as unmistakably as he had done. She just would not be present when he arrived. She would be up in her room. Let him speak to Papa and Christopher to his heart's content. He need not say one single word to her!

"Girl! You are not giving me your attention!" Sir Joseph's voice sounded sharply.

Ann gave a little start.

"What is wrong, child? Are you ill? I do not think you are looking very well, and that is quite understandable. Christopher, how does your sister appear to you?"

"A little pale, I should say, Father. I think I share her feelings. The prospect of Blayde's visit, after all the damage he has done, does not fill me with any delight. Are you sure that I must be included in your discussions with him?"

"Well, of course, you must, you imbecile! It stands to reason if you are to be the subject of our conversation, your interest specifically, you have got to attend his lordship. What would he think of you, otherwise?"

"That I do not care a farthing's worth for him, and find his absence a blessing and his presence a curse!"

"That will be quite enough out of you, Mr. Keating! Has it ever occurred to you, either one of you, that Lord Blayde may have come to conclude that he owes us something for the embarrassment he has caused us?"

Retorted Ann: "I should think, in that event, it was *my* interest and not Christopher's that was involved; yet he has not a word to say about me."

"That is quite understandable, my dear," said Sir Joseph, with a kindly smile. "You see, the only way he could make amends to you directly would be to marry you, and that, you will admit, would be something drastic."

"Hah!" sniffed Ann. "I would not marry the likes of his lordship were he the last man on earth!"

With that she rose from the table and rushed out of the room, sobbing.

"I say, Papa, what is going on with her?" asked Christopher.

Sir Joseph, his eyes still on the door through

which Ann had disappeared, sighed. "I fear, my lad, that I sadly underestimated the damage that gentleman has done to this family. I pray that his visit tomorrow will be brief and unexceptional."

CHAPTER 17

Slumber drifted away from Ann so subtly that she never realized she had been awake for long minutes until it came to her that she was staring up at the canopy in the murky light of after-dawning. For how long she lay in that state, she did not know, nor did she attempt to recall, for within her there was a burgeoning surge of excitement.

Henry was to come calling that day and despite her resolve of yesterday, she knew that she would be on hand to greet him. It would have been beyond bearing to be in the same house with him and not make some attempt to catch a glimpse of him. She had not seen him for three days and she was impelled to determine how much he had changed in that time. Perhaps now he was rested, perhaps now his surliness was dissipated and they could have a little conversation between them, before he went in to sit with her father and Christopher.

Perhaps not—but she was filled with an irresistable impulse to make the attempt. It would add up to nothing, she was sure, but when she was away in Cheltenham, or even for the months longer that they might spend in Tewin, she would have this last memory of him to keep her company.

It was odd, so very odd, that she should feel this way about Henry. They had not been at all on warm terms from the beginning. And things between them had grown more frigid with every passing moment, winding up in angry discord so that they were barely civil with each other. Surely Fate was now taking pity on them and providing this one last opportunity to reestablish a friendship that had died aborning.

Then, too, there was the purpose of Henry's call. If he had felt coolness to her, his manner to Christopher had been sheer ice. That he should have the least concern for her brother was beyond imagination. Again the thought that his purpose was not cordial came to mind, and it made her nervous.

Yes, it was of the first importance that she get to talk with Henry before he went in to her father. If she could gain but a hint of his intention, she could make an appeal to his finer nature— At that point her thinking plunged into confusion. What could he be at? What could she say to him? How divert him from wreaking his spite upon poor Christopher? If anyone deserved such punishment, it was she—and that is what she would have to say to him.

Contemplating such a course with Henry brought

moisture to her eyes. She prayed it would not be necessary.

But sleep now was far removed from her and she could no longer lie idly abed. She had much to do this morning before Henry arrived. The house must be made spotless, and that must call for her undivided attention as she directed the maids in their tasks. And it had to be accomplished with dispatch, for there was the grooming of her own person. This one time, she wished to appear before Henry dressed to perfection, her toilet impeccable.

All of it had to be done well before Henry was expected so that she would have time to see her father and Christopher safely stowed in the library while she waited in the front room for those few moments alone with Henry, those few moments she hoped to be able to cherish for the rest of her days.

Ann came into the front room which served the Keatings as the drawing room with her cheeks flushed, the only sign of the high tide of agitation flooding her breast. Very composedly, she went over to the sofa and, carefully spreading her skirts, sat down in the middle of it.

She was a little out of breath, as much from the morning exertions as from anxiety. It had taken a bit of doing to get the servants—they had so few—to make everything presentable, and to see to it that Sir Joseph was in faultless attire and settled in the library for his forthcoming interview. Christopher had proved a problem, and she had had need of her father's authority to bring him to heel. With a bad grace, he finally acceded to her demand that he don his best clothes for the occasion.

It was all done and the Keatings were now quite prepared to receive his lordship in unexceptional style. As for herself, after all she had been through this morning, she was not sure what sort of appearance she would make. Her hair had proved nigh unmanageable this day of all days, and it had taken all her cleverness, together with the assistance of the youngest of the maids, to dress it reasonably properly. And, wouldn't you know it, her best gown proved to have a fallen hem, and that had to be quickly stitched up. For such company as she was expecting, mere pinning would never have been satisfactory.

Then the gown gave her pause, too. It was her best dress and, naturally, it was the very one that she had worn the night of Almack's, which explained how the hem might have got torn; but Henry had already seen her in it! But, as it was not only her very best gown but also so far above her everyday wear, she had no choice in the matter.

It all went to making her feel not quite up-to-the-nines and she could have cried in her frustration. However that luxury must be denied to her, or she would have had all of the trouble of having to repair the ravages of tears. It was far too close to the time that Henry might arrive to allow for such nonsense.

Henry, too, came in for a bit of castigation. He could have appointed a definite hour instead of indicating some vague time in the morning. She was having to guess at his arrival, but felt fairly certain that he must make his appearance sometime between ten and eleven o'clock—although as he was a Londoner, there was truly no saying.

But now she could at least rest and restore her composure to something like normal. Her heart was fluttering, and her throat and mouth felt exceptionally dry, so that she was beginning to fear that she would not be able to say a word. But that worry was put into abeyance as Christopher, looking very neat and trim, but at the same time very determined, came into the room.

As he marched up to the front door, she demanded: "Christopher, where are you going?"

He turned, with his hand on the doornob, and said, a most supercilious expression on his face: "I am going out."

"Christopher, I will not have it! We are expecting a guest, and he may arrive at any moment!"

"Devil I care! This place has become a madhouse, and I am in need of a breath of air—"

"Christopher, don't you dare to leave! How will it look if his lordship should arrive in your absence?"

Christopher cocked his head and, with a bit of a leer, replied: "As you are looking particularly handsome this morning, dear sister, I suspect that his lordship will never miss me."

"Oh, do you think that I look all right, truly?" It was almost a plea as she raised a hand to pat an imaginary, unruly curl into place.

"My dear, I have never seen you look better. Now, by your leave or no, I am for a breath of air."

With that he opened the door and stepped outside. He never shut it but stuck his head back in and said: "Brace yourself, pet. I believe that is his nibs about to descend upon us."

If Ann had been anxious before, now her agitation threatened to overcome her. Henry would be at the door at any second and there was Christopher, hanging on the knob like a monkey and grinning at her like an idiot. It was all wrong. The little conversation she had planned would never take place. She might just as well have stayed up in her room after all.

Henry entered the room, looking quite composed, his linen sparkling white, his costume for riding about the country, richly made, but modest in appearance à la Brummell. He handed his crop and his gloves to Christopher who blinked in puzzlement for a moment before he deposited them upon a chair next to the door.

"Greetings, Miss Keating. Christopher," he said, and then stood waiting.

"You come in good time, your lordship. We are all of us awaiting you."

"I pray I have not kept you waiting long, Miss Keating."

"Not at all, your lordship," replied Ann, thinking, Oh, how cold he is! Not realizing that her posture was no warmer toward him.

Then, as the conversation seemed to have died a thorough death, she offered: "My father awaits you in his study. I will show you the way, your lordship."

"Thank you, Miss Keating."

Henry followed Ann into the library, trailed by Christopher. Then, as Ann started to withdraw, he turned and asked: "I say, Miss Keating, will you not be joining us?"

"I am sure that nothing you will be discussing concerns me, your lordship. I should only be in the way."

At this point Henry's attention was dragged away by Sir Joseph arising to bid him welcome. Ann slipped out of the room, shutting the door behind her.

She felt thoroughly defeated. The ice was still there. All the strained anticipation that she had suffered through the morning was now gone leaving her feeling quite drained. Henry was not at all the person she had remembered.

It was not that he was changed, it was just that his coolness was now something quite real. From the moment he had stepped into the house, there was a guarded look in his eyes. It was as though he had no wish to even look at her and needs must keep his face slightly turned from her. His query about her joining in the conversation was merely a moment's recollection of the right thing to say. Oh, she could cry!

But precisely over what, she was not sure. It was a piece of foolishness that she should have ever been so aroused at the prospect of Henry's coming. Now that he had come, she could see that there was nothing changed between them. What a silly girl she had been!

No, there was no point in tears, she thought as she made her way up to her room. Henry was not worth crying over, and it was just as well. Why, if she had gone on in this missish fashion, who knows? She might have fallen in love with him!

By the time she came into her chamber, she understood full well that that was exactly what she had already done—and she fell upon her bed, bathing her pillow with the tears of heartbreak.

After awhile, Ann arose from the bed and dried her eyes. If ever a female received a just punishment for exceptional behavior, she had, and there was no point in carrying on about it.

Had she ever given the least bit of sober consideration to it, she would have realized that a connection with so high and mighty a one as Henry Vassall, Viscount Blayde, was quite beyond the expectations of a mere Ann Keating. The trouble was that she had no chance to give any thought to it at all, actually. Although she had found the Viscount an attractive gentleman, she had not intended, in any way whatsoever, to try to put him into her pocket. There was this little frolicsome enterprise that they had entered into, and that was all there was to it—or ought to have been. For her suddenly to discover that she was head over heels in love with the fellow was singularly unfair. It was poor consolation to know that she deserved a punishment. She would have much preferred whatever her father had in mind to mete out to her, which was to be something additional to her discomfort, she was sure.

In any case, there was nothing left to her but to lick her wounds and retire with resignation. Ultimately, the disgrace must pass. The trouble with that was, it seemed to her that resignation was all she had been doing ever since the fateful moment of her discovery by Lady Jersey. It was bound to be a bit of a bore. And that must call for more resignation!

Ann smiled to herself. The situation was become

a little ridiculous, she thought. Oh, if only Henry had a sense of humor beyond that of playing boy's tricks on people, what fun they could have, laughing over the entire experience.

Ann sighed in resignation just as there was a knocking upon her door. She went over to it and opened it to admit Christopher.

He came into the room smiling. "I say, Ann, why are you all tucked away up here? Henry is about to depart. He seems to be anxious to speak with you before he leaves."

"Henry? You are suddenly on close terms with Viscount Blayde."

"I think I had got him down all wrong. Actually, once you get to know the chap, he is a bit of all right, don't you know?"

"No, I do not know. How comes this sudden change in your feelings toward his lordship? You were at each other's throats the last time."

"Oh that? Well, it is all quite behind us. We neither of us understood what it was all about, you see. He is bound to make amends to us, and being a good sort myself, I made no bones about accepting his generous offer."

"What offer?" asked Ann, frowning.

"That is why he came calling, my dear. He has a wish to take me into his service. He is sadly in need for someone to look after his affairs and thought I might do it quite nicely, once I completed my sojourn at Oxford. I agreed, of course, and so he is going to see to it that I do not have to wait 'til next year before I go back. He is going to speak with the Chancellor, and as he has the very best connections, it ought not take too long. Awfully nice of him, you will agree."

Absently, Ann replied: "Quite. Is that all you talked about?"

"All? I should think so! Is not that enough?"

"I dare say. But I should like to know if, by any chance, he men—er, I was mentioned."

Christopher looked genuinely puzzled. "No, not a bit. Oh, I see what it is you are driving at! You think that perhaps his nose is out of joint over that messy business. My dear, I can assure you it is not. He was very amiable, and we were able to speak quite freely together, Henry and I. He is going to call me Chris. Actually begged the privilege as a favor to him. I say!"

Christopher grinned as he looked off into space, savoring the memory.

"Where is he now?"

"Henry is speaking with Father in the drawing room. If you are going to see him, you had better hurry."

"How do I look?" asked Ann, anxiously, as she presented herself for his approval.

"Quite well, I am sure. Come, let us not keep Henry waiting."

"Here she is, Henry," said Christopher, brightly, as he and Ann came into the room.

A smile started on Henry's lips but quickly died away as he nodded to her.

Then a most uncomfortable interlude followed. Apparently, Sir Joseph and Henry had just been exchanging talk and now that Ann was come, no one seemed to know how to revive the conversation.

Sir Joseph, after studying his daughter for a moment, said: "I am feeling a little fatigued. It has been a most interesting morning, my lord, and

I am sure that all hard feelings between us have been thoroughly dissipated. By your leave, I should like to withdraw—and have a chat with my son over his good fortune. Why do you not go out into the garden. Ann! Do not stand there! I am sure that his lordship will be pleased for a sight of a well-tended garden before he must return to the City where such is a great rarity."

Ann doubted the wisdom of her father's suggestion, but etiquette demanded that she second the offer. She was quite prepared to hear it declined.

"Yes, that would be rather nice, thank you."

Before Ann could recover from her surprise, her father stunned her further by suggesting: "Ann, my dear, see if you can prevail upon his lordship to join us in a small repast. It would be no trouble at all to set another cover."

"Thank you, Sir Joseph, but I shall have to be running on. It has been a genuine pleasure to speak with you and Christopher. I shall let you know how things are arranged at the earliest possible moment."

With that, he opened the door for Ann to pass outside before him.

Ann was at a loss for words. There were so many things she wished she could ask Henry, but although he seemed content to walk along beside her in the garden, he was not making any attempt at conversation. She did not know what to make of his attitude. He was pleasant enough with her father, as she had just witnessed, but now he had naught to say.

Finally, she said: "Christopher has informed me

of your generosity, my lord. I could hope that this gesture of yours signals the end of animosity between us, too."

He turned to her and exclaimed: "Oh, I say that is not at all true! I never entertained any but the kindest feelings for you, Ann. It is I who have been wondering at your coldness to me of late. I mean to say I have been put to the greatest trouble, trying to make up for the mess we got ourselves into, and in the process have been made thoroughly aware of the nobility of your father. He is a proud gentleman and a gentleman to be proud of. I admit that I took Chris for a good-for-nothing, especially after I had learned that he had been sent down. But as son to your father, there has got to be excellent blood in him. That made me think on the business rather deeply, and I came to a conclusion that I found quite shocking.

"Both Countesses were in the right for dealing with me so sharply, and it stood to reason that your father must have, for the very same reason, nurtured a pure hatred for me and what I had done to you. I had been a cad of the lowest sort, getting you into all that was scandalous—"

"But Henry, you could not have done it had I not gone along with it—"

"I pray you will not interrupt me, girl. It is hard enough to get all this out in the open as it is, and it is the very purpose of my calling upon you."

Ann was too shocked to be able to say a word, but her heart went on at such a pace that she probably would not have had the breath anyway.

"Yes," Henry went on, "it was quite base of me to inveigle you into it. I asked myself the question: Suppose you had been Horatia, would I have dared to place you in such jeopardy? Of course, I would not! And for the very obvious reason that she is my sister and I honor her and deem it my duty to protect her. Ann, I showed you no such honor, and that was unspeakable in me. I have got to make it up to you. Please to command me."

"Oh Henry, I care not for such nonsense. I am sure that your sister would never have allowed herself to be demeaned in the manner that I chose. I am equally at fault for having permitted it, nay wished it! I am just so pleased that we are no longer at arm's length with each other. I would have your friendship, and I thought that I had lost it."

"I assure you, my dear, there was never any danger of that. Yes, you are quite right, it never would have entered Horatia's head to go off to Almack's without a voucher. She is a most proper young lady, which you are not, I am happy to say. I mean, you will admit that for all of the fuss, still it was quite a lark."

"Yes, I dare say. But there were times when I wished we had not begun it, and now that it is over, I am quite relieved. It was something of an ordeal, you know."

He chuckled. "Yes, wasn't it, though! But, Ann, you have not said what I must do to make it up to you."

"Truly, Henry, there is naught within reason, not that I think it is incumbent on you at all. What you are doing for Christopher must make up for all."

"No, you misunderstand. What I am doing for Christopher, I am doing for myself. That has nothing to do with you. Now, is there anything you want? Is there anything I can do that would please you beyond measure?"

"Truly, Henry, there is nothing needed. The situation is so extraordinary that it does not bear thinking on. As my father put it, and I assure you he was joking when he said it: It would take nothing short of marriage to repair the business—and you can see how utterly impossible that is."

He turned his head sharply to look at her.

"I beg your pardon, Henry," she said, quickly. "I assure you it was only in jest. In fact, I do recall that my answer to him at that point—and I was highly wroth with you, being under the impression that you detested me—that I should not have married you were you the last man on earth," she said, laughing rather weakly. It did not seem at all funny to her.

Apparently it did not seem at all funny to Henry either. His look changed into a glare of anger.

He turned to her and took her roughly by the arms, bringing her so close to him that their faces were almost touching.

Breathing heavily, he growled: "So that is how it is with you, Miss Keating, is it? Then I had best take advantage of any opportunity I can find. Perhaps I might even manage to change your mind about that!"

Ann was powerless in the strong grip of his hands, not that she might have tried to prevent him. His lips came crushingly down upon hers and his arms wrapped themselves about her, pressing her close, close to him.

Oh! Henry, I want you so! was what she wanted

to exclaim, but her lips, her mouth, her entire being were so wrapped up in Henry's caress, she could only clutch him to her with all her strength, the lightest of moans issuing from her throat.

CHAPTER 18

"Unhand my daughter, you cur!"

They broke apart so quickly that Ann almost fell. Henry grabbed her and held her close to him.

"Sir Joseph, I bid you to be calm," said Henry, with a little smile playing about his lips.

Ann felt awful. Once again she had managed to hurt her father. Oh, how unthinking she could be! Allowing herself to fall into the arms of a man who had already admitted he did not honor her was unspeakably base.

"Ann, go to your room! At once, do you hear!"

She made a move to obey, but Henry's arm about her waist tightened and she could not free herself.

"Now, Sir Joseph, you are taking your fences much too quickly and are headed for a bruising fall," said Henry. "I think we have got something to discuss."

"I, sir, think not! Now I bid you unhand my daughter and depart the premises at once. I have never in all my life—"

"Quite. As you have but the one daughter, it is quite true that this has never occurred before—unless she is already affianced."

Sir Joseph's face, which had been glowing with anger, changed completely to an expression of incredulity.

"What the devil do you mean, sir?"

"I mean that, if *I* have anything to say to it, Ann is going to be my wife, sir."

"You would marry Ann, after all the trouble that she gave you?"

"I think we are all agreed, Sir Joseph, that I had as much to do with it as she did. Can you imagine the sort of frolics that we shall dream up between us when we are wed?"

For the first time, Sir Joseph grinned. "I—I beg your pardon, my lord. I quite misunderstood—"

"Indeed, you did. Now, I must trouble you to leave us, sir. I have still to understand if my darling approves of my offer, and I shall need time to convince her. I was hard at work at it when you interrupted us."

Now Sir Joseph broke into laughter. Without a word he turned on his heel and went back into the house.

Henry immediately whipped Ann about and began to take up where he had left off, but Ann stopped him with a light hand on his lips.

"Oh, sir, pity me!" she pleaded. "My hard-hearted father has abandoned his only daughter, leaving her at the mercy of a wolf in viscount's clothing."

"Yes, he did. Now wasn't that rather nice of the old boy?"

But Ann was not in any mood for talking. Her eyes were closed and her lips were raised. Henry saw and obeyed.

Let COVENTRY Give You
A Little Old-Fashioned Romance

- ☐ THE BLUE DIAMOND   50213 $1.50
  by Joan Smith

- ☐ IN MY LADY'S CHAMBER   50214 $1.50
  by Elizabeth Neff Walker

- ☐ A SEASON ABROAD   50215 $1.50
  by Rebecca Baldwin

- ☐ THE QUEEN'S QUADRILLE   50212 $1.50
  by Georgina Grey

- ☐ MY LORDS, LADIES
  AND MARJORIE   50216 $1.50
  by Marion Chesney

- ☐ GALLANT LADY   50217 $1.50
  by Elizabeth Chater

Buy them at your local bookstore or use this handy coupon for ordering.

COLUMBIA BOOK SERVICE
32275 Mally Road, P.O. Box FB, Madison Heights, MI 48071

Please send me the books I have checked above. Orders for less than 5 books must include 75¢ for the first book and 25¢ for each additional book to cover postage and handling. Orders for 5 books or more postage is FREE. Send check or money order only. Allow 3-4 weeks for delivery.

Cost $_____   Name_____

Sales tax*_____   Address_____

Postage _____   City_____

Total $_____   State_____ Zip_____

*The government requires us to collect sales tax in all states except AK, DE, MT, NH and OR.

Prices and availability subject to change without notice.   **8212**

ROMANCE From Fawcett Books